## 'I'd like to return to Kallos within the hour.'

Knowing she was sounding stupid, Talia couldn't keep herself from repeating him yet again. 'Kallos…?'

'My home,' Angelos clarified. 'Did you not read the advertisement I placed, Miss Di Sione?'

Talia dragged a deep breath into her lungs and tried to force her mind to clear. She straightened, putting the glass of juice on the desk with a clink. 'Mr—Kyrie Mena, I'm afraid this has all got a little out of hand…'

She felt another blush rising as Angelos's eyebrows snapped together in irritated confusion. If she told him the real reason for her being here now, he'd be utterly furious. Angelos Mena would be enraged to learn she actually had no intention or interest in being his daughter's nanny.

Except…could she really say that?

Talia's gaze slid to Sofia, who was watching her anxiously, her dark hair swinging in front of her face to hide her scarred cheek.

Talia's heart twisted hard in sympathy, just as it had when she'd first laid eyes on this girl. Sofia wanted her to come, and it was only for six weeks. And surely in six weeks she'd find an opportunity to ask Angelos about the book—even get him to give her the _____ _____ to hel_____ hip.

Wh_____

# The Billionaire's Legacy

*A search for truth and the promise of passion!*

For nearly sixty years
Italian billionaire Giovanni Di Sione has kept
a shocking secret. Now, nearing the end of his days,
he wants his grandchildren to know their true heritage.

He sends them each on a journey to find his
'Lost Mistresses'—a collection of love tokens
and the only remaining evidence of his lost identity,
his lost history…his lost love.

With each item collected the Di Sione siblings take one
step closer to the truth…and embark on a passionate
journey that none could have expected!

Find out what happens in

**The Billionaire's Legacy**

**Collect all 8 volumes!**

# A DI SIONE FOR THE GREEK'S PLEASURE

BY
KATE HEWITT

First Published in Great Britain 2016
By Mills & Boon, an imprint of HarperCollins*Publishers*
1 London Bridge Street, London, SE1 9GF

© 2016 Harlequin Books S.A.

Special thanks and acknowledgment are given to Kate Hewitt for her
contribution to The Billionaire's Legacy series.

ISBN: 978-0-263-91663-8

Our policy is to use papers that are natural, renewable and recyclable
products and made from wood grown in sustainable forests. The logging
and manufacturing processes conform to the legal environmental
regulations of the country of origin.

Printed and bound in Spain
by CPI, Barcelona

After spending three years as a die-hard New Yorker, **Kate Hewitt** now lives in a small village in the English Lake District with her husband, their five children and a golden retriever. In addition to writing intensely emotional stories she loves reading, baking and playing chess with her son—she has yet to win against him, but she continues to try. Learn more about Kate at kate-hewitt.com.

### Books by Kate Hewitt

### Mills & Boon Modern Romance

*Moretti's Marriage Command*
*Inherited by Ferranti*
*Kholodov's Last Mistress*
*The Undoing of de Luca*

### Secret Heirs of Billionaires

*Demetriou Demands His Child*

### One Night With Consequences

*Larenzo's Christmas Baby*

### The Marakaios Brides

*The Marakaios Marriage*
*The Marakaios Baby*

### The Chatsfield

*Virgin's Sweet Rebellion*

### Rivals to the Crown of Kadar

*Captured by the Sheikh*
*Commanded by the Sheikh*

### The Diomedi Heirs

*The Prince She Never Knew*
*A Queen for the Taking?*

Visit the Author Profile page
at millsandboon.co.uk for more titles.

# CHAPTER ONE

'I WANT YOU to do something for me.'

Natalia Di Sione smiled at her grandfather as she adjusted the blanket over his legs and sat down across from him. Even though it was the hottest part of a June day, Giovanni Di Sione still shivered slightly in the wind coming off the Long Island Sound.

'Anything, Nonno,' Natalia said, using the name she'd called him since she was a little girl.

Giovanni gave her a whimsical smile as he shook his head. 'You are so quick to agree, Talia, yet you do not know what I am going to ask.'

'You know I'd do anything for you.' Giovanni had raised Talia and her siblings after her parents had died in a car accident when she, as the youngest of seven, had been little more than a baby. He was father, mother and grandfather rolled into one, and since she'd been living on the Di Sione estate with him for the last seven years, he was also the closest thing she had to a confidant and best friend.

She knew some of her older siblings had retained a little distance from their hardworking and sometimes remote grandfather, but in the last seven years Talia had embraced him wholly. He'd offered her refuge when she'd crawled back here, wounded in both body and mind. He'd been her salvation.

'Anything, Talia?' Giovanni asked, arching one eyebrow in wry challenge. 'Even, perhaps, leave the estate?'

She laughed lightly. 'Surely you wouldn't ask me to do something as terrible as that.' She pretended to shudder, although the truth was just the prospect of stepping foot outside the lavish gated estate made her insides clench in fear. She liked her ivory tower, the security of knowing she was protected, behind gates, *safe*. Because she knew what it was like not to feel safe, to feel as if your very life hung by a single, slender thread, and she refused ever to feel that way again…even if it meant living like a prisoner.

She left the villa at most only a few times a year, usually to visit one of her siblings or attend a private viewing at the occasional art exhibition nearby. She avoided cities and even Long Island's Gold Coast's small, well-heeled towns, and restricted travel to short jaunts in a chauffeured car.

When Giovanni suggested Talia get out more, she insisted she preferred a quiet life on the estate, with its sprawling villa, rolling manicured lawns and the winking blue of the Long Island Sound in the distance. Why, she teased her grandfather, did she need to go anywhere else?

Giovanni was kind enough not to push. Yet Talia knew he was concerned about her isolation, even if he never said it. She saw how worry often shadowed his eyes or drew his bushy eyebrows together as he watched her pottering about the villa.

'You know I do not have long left, Talia,' Giovanni said now, and she merely nodded, not trusting her voice. A few months ago Giovanni had been given a year to live. Considering he was ninety-eight years old and had already beaten cancer once, nearly twenty years ago, a year was a long time. But it wasn't long enough for Talia.

She couldn't imagine the villa without Giovanni, his gentle smiles and wise words, his often silent yet steady presence. The huge, elegant rooms would seem emptier than ever, the estate yawning in all directions, inhabited only by her and its skeleton staff. She hated the thought, and so her mind skittered away from it.

'So what would you like me to do?' Talia asked. 'Paint your portrait?' For the last few years she had built up a small but thriving career painting portraits. For her twenty-first birthday Giovanni had given her a studio on the grounds of the estate, a small, shingled building with a glorious view of the Sound. Clients came to her studio to sit for their portraits, and she enjoyed the social inter-action as well as the creative work, all in the secure envi-ronment she craved.

'A portrait?' Giovanni chuckled. 'Who would like to see an old man such as me? No, *cara*, I'd like something else. I'd like you to find something for me.' He sat back in his chair, his gnarled hands folded in his lap, and watched her, waiting.

'Find something?' Talia leaned forward, surprised and curious, as well as more than a little apprehensive. She recognised that knowing gleam in her grandfather's eyes, the way he went silent, content to let her be the one to ask. 'Have you lost something, Nonno?'

'I have lost many things over the years,' Giovanni an-swered. Talia heard a touch of sad whimsy in his voice, saw how his face took on a faraway look. A faint smile curved his mouth, as if he was remembering something sweet or perhaps poignant. Then he turned back to Talia. 'I want you to find one of them. One of my Lost Mistresses.'

Talia knew about Giovanni's Lost Mistresses; it was a tale cloaked in mystery that she'd grown up on: a collec-tion of precious objects that Giovanni had carried with him into the new world, when he'd emigrated from Italy as a young man. He'd been forced to sell them off one by one to survive, although he'd loved them all dearly. He'd always refused to say any more than that, claiming an old man must have some secrets. Talia suspected Giovanni had many secrets, and now, with a flicker of curiosity, she wondered if he would tell her at least one of them.

'One of your Lost Mistresses?' she repeated. 'But you've never actually said what they are. Which one is it?'

'A book, a very special book, and one that will be very difficult to find.'

She raised her eyebrows. 'And you think *I* can find it?'

'Yes, I do. I trust your intelligence and ingenuity, Talia. Your creativity. It shines from your soul.'

She laughed and shook her head, embarrassed and touched. Her grandfather did not often speak so sentimentally, but she knew that the years weighed on him now and she suspected he felt the need to say things he'd kept hidden for so long.

'What kind of book?' she asked.

'A book of love poems, written by an anonymous poet from the Mediterranean. It is called *Il Libro d'Amore*.'

*'The Book of Love,'* Talia translated. 'Are there many copies of it available?'

'A handful perhaps, but the one I possessed was unlike any other, a first edition with a cover of hand-tooled leather. It is truly unique.'

'And yet you think I can find it?' Talia said, doubt creeping into her voice. She'd been envisioning doing a quick Internet search, maybe tracking the book down through a used book dealer. But of course Giovanni could do that himself. He'd bought a tablet years ago, and innovative entrepreneur that he'd always been, he regularly surfed the Internet.

But of course he wanted her to do something far more

difficult. Something far more important. And she knew she didn't want to let him down.

Her grandfather hadn't asked much of her over the years; he'd graciously given her her own private living quarters on his estate when she'd been just nineteen years old and barely able to cope. He'd never pushed her too hard to get out or to try new things, and he'd made her career as an artist possible without ever having to leave the villa. She owed a lot to her *nonno*.

'Yes, I want you to find that particular book,' he said, smiling sadly. 'There is an inscription on the inside cover: "Dearest Lucia, For ever in my heart, always. B.A."' His voice choked a little and he looked down, blinking rapidly, before he gazed back up at Talia with his usual whimsical smile. 'That is how you will know it is the right one.'

'Who is Lucia?' Talia felt oddly moved by the inscription, as well as her grandfather's obvious and unusual emotion. 'And who is B.A.? Were they friends of yours?'

'You could say that, yes. They were very dear to me, and they loved each other very much.' Giovanni sat back, adjusting the blanket over his legs, his face pale. Talia had been noticing how easily he tired lately; clearly their conversation had worn him out. 'But that,' Giovanni said, a note of finality in his voice, 'is a story for another time.'

'But what happened to the book?' Talia asked. 'Did you sell it when you reached America?'

'No, I never took it to America. I left it behind, and that is why it will be difficult to find. But I think you are capable, Talia. Even if finding it may take you on a journey in more ways than one.'

'A journey…' Talia pressed her lips together. She was pretty sure that finding this book was her grandfather's way of getting her off the estate, out into life. She knew he'd been wanting her to spread her wings for some time now, and she'd always resisted, insisted she was happy here on the estate. How could she not be? She had everything she wanted right here. She didn't need more, didn't want adventure or excitement. Not as she once had.

*Because look where that had got her.*

'Nonno...' she began, and Giovanni shook a finger at her in gentle admonition.

'You are not going to refuse an old man a dying wish?'

'Don't say that—'

'*Cara*, it's true. And I wish to have this book very much. To turn its fragile pages and read of how love surpasses any glory, any tragedy...' His voice choked once more and Talia bit her lip as guilt flooded through her.

How on earth could she even consider refusing her grandfather's request, all out of her own selfish fear? How could she say no to Giovanni, her *nonno* who had taken care of her since she was a baby? Who had been as both mother and father, and lived with her these last seven years, accepting her limitations, loving her anyway?

'I'll try, Nonno,' she said finally, and Giovanni leaned forward to rest his bony hand on top of hers.

'I know you will, *cara*,' he said, his voice hoarse as he smiled at her. 'I know you will try your hardest. And you will succeed.'

'There is one more woman to see you, Kyrie Mena.'

Angelos Mena looked up from his desk and the stack of CVs he'd scanned and then discarded. None of the young women he'd interviewed that afternoon had been remotely appropriate for the position. In fact, he suspected they'd been more interested in cosying up to him than getting to know his daughter, Sofia, just as the last three nannies had been.

His mouth thinning in disgust, he ran his hand through

his hair and then shook his head. 'One more? But that should be all.' He tapped the discarded pile of papers on his desk. 'I have no more CVs.'

His assistant, Eleni, spread her hands in helpless ignorance. 'She has been waiting here for several hours, saying she needs to see you.'

'She has tenacity, then, at least.' He pushed away from the desk. 'You might as well send her in.'

With a click of heels Eleni left his office and Angelos rose to stand by the floor-to-ceiling window that overlooked Athens. Tension knotted the muscles of his shoulders and made his temples throb. He really hadn't needed the complication of his new nanny delaying her start by six weeks. Finding an acceptable temporary replacement was a challenge he did not relish, especially considering that not one of the dozen women he'd interviewed today had been suitable.

Some had had experience, yes, but when he'd called Sofia in to see if his daughter approved, she'd resisted the women's cloying attempts at friendship. Even Angelos had been able to see how patently false they were. He'd noticed how several of the women hadn't wanted to look at Sofia; several others had stared. Both reactions had made his daughter shrink back in shame, and the injustice of it made Angelos seethe with fury. His daughter had nothing to be ashamed about.

Not like he did.

'Mr Menos?'

Angelos turned around to see a slender young woman standing in the doorway. She looked pale but resolute, her sandy brown hair tousled, the simple pink cotton sundress she wore hopelessly wrinkled. Angelos frowned at the sight of her dishevelment. Clearly she did not dress to impress.

'And you are?' he asked, his tone deliberately curt.

'I'm sorry…um…*signomi*…but I don't speak…*den*…uh…*milau*…' She stammered, a flush washing over her face, making her hazel eyes seem luminous in her freckled, heart-shaped face.

'You don't speak Greek?' Angelos finished for her in flawless, clipped English. 'And yet my daughter's only language is Greek. How…interesting, Miss…?' He arched an eyebrow, smiling coldly. He did not have time for another completely unsuitable candidate to witter her way through an interview. Better to have her scurry away now.

'Miss Natalia Di Sione,' the woman said. She straightened her spine, fire flashing in those golden-green eyes, surprising Angelos. The woman had spirit. 'And actually, your daughter does speak a bit of English, if you are referring to the young girl who has been sitting outside the office all afternoon.'

Angelos's eyebrows snapped together. 'You have been talking to her?'

'Yes.' She eyed him uncertainly, the tip of her tongue coming out to moisten her lips. Angelos acknowledged the tiny gesture with an uncomfortable tightening in his insides that he resolutely ignored. 'Was I not supposed to?'

'That is neither here nor there.' He tapped the pile of CVs on his desk. 'You have not provided me with a CV, Miss Di Sione.'

'A CV?' She looked blank and irritation rose within him. She was clearly unsuitable and hopelessly unprepared. A change from the hard polish of the last few candidates, but irritating nonetheless.

'I am afraid I do not have time to indulge you, Miss Di Sione,' he said. 'You are clearly completely unsuitable for the position.'

'The position…' For a moment she looked utterly flummoxed, her forehead crinkling, her mouth pursing. Angelos moved from around his desk and towards the door. As he passed her he caught a whiff of her scent, something clean and simple. Almonds, perhaps. He reached for the door handle. 'Thank you for your time, Miss Di Sione, but I prefer you don't waste mine.'

'But I haven't even talked to you yet,' she protested, turning around to face him. She tucked her unruly hair behind her ears, drawing his attention to the long, golden-brown strands, her small, perfectly formed ears.

*Good grief.* He was staring at her *ears*. What was wrong with him?

His gaze dropped from her ears to the shoulders that she'd thrown back, and now he noticed her slender yet gently curving body. He yanked his gaze back upwards to her face and determinedly kept it there.

'I've learned enough from our brief conversation. You have no CV, you wear a crumpled dress to a job interview—'

'I just got off a plane,' she shot back, and her gaze widened. 'A *job* interview...'

'You are here,' Angelos bit out, sarcasm edging every word, 'to interview for the temporary position as nanny?'

'Nanny? To your daughter?'

'Who else?' Angelos exploded, and she nodded quickly.

'Of course, of course. I... I apologise for not having my CV with me.' The tip of her tongue touched her lips again and Angelos looked away. 'I only heard about this... position recently. Could you...could you tell me exactly what it entails?'

He frowned, wanting to dismiss her, needing to, because he knew she was completely unsuitable. And yet... something about her clear gaze, the stiffness of her spine, made him hesitate. 'You would care for my eight-year-old daughter, Sofia. The nanny I hired has had to look after her ill mother, and she cannot start until the end of August. Therefore I require a replacement for the six weeks until then. This was all in the advertisement?'

She nodded slowly, her hazel eyes wide, sweeping him with that unsettlingly clear gaze. 'Yes, of course. I remember now.'

His breath released in an impatient hiss. 'Do you have any child-care experience, Miss Di Sione?'

'Please, call me Talia. And the answer to that is no.'

He stared at her in disbelief. 'None?' She shook her head, her wavy hair falling about her face once more. She tucked it behind her ears, smiling at him almost impishly, and Angelos's simmering temper came to a boil. She had an unfortunate amount of gall to demand an interview with absolutely no experience to recommend her. He shook his head. 'You are, as I suspected from the moment you entered this office, wasting my time.'

Talia Di Sione blinked, recoiling a little bit at his tone. Angelos felt no sympathy. Why had the woman come here? She had no CV, no experience, no chance whatsoever. Surely she should have realised that.

'Perhaps you should ask your daughter if I wasted her time,' she said quietly, and then Angelos stilled.

Talia watched Angelos Mena's pupils flare, his mouth tighten. Animosity and impatience rolled off the man in waves, along with something else. Something disturbing… a power like a magnetic force, making her realise how dangerous this man could be. And yet she didn't feel remotely threatened, despite all the challenges she'd faced today, leaving her emotionally raw and physically exhausted.

Angelos folded his arms, the fabric of his suit stretching across impressive biceps. If he didn't look so utterly forbidding, Talia would have considered Angelos Mena a handsome man. Actually, she would have considered him a stunning, sexy and potently virile man. His tall, powerful body was encased in that very expensive-looking suit, and the silver and gold links of a designer wristwatch glinted from one powerful wrist. Crisp dark hair cut very short framed a chiselled face with straight slashes of eyebrows and deep brown eyes that had been glowering at her like banked coals for the entirety of this unfortunate interview.

Not that she'd been expecting to be *interviewed*. She'd been waiting outside Angelos Mena's office for four hours, hoping for a chance to meet him and ask him about *Il Libro d'Amore*. It had taken her several weeks of painstaking research to track down the precious book to the man standing in front of her, and she still wasn't positive he had it in his possession. The Internet had taken her only so far, and when she'd called Mena Consultancy several times she'd been unable to reach the man himself. She'd left a few vague messages with his PA, wanting to explain what she was looking for in an actual conversation, but judging by Angelos Mena's attitude now, she didn't think he'd received any of them. Her name clearly hadn't rung any bells, and it had only taken ten seconds in the man's presence to realise that a simple conversation probably wouldn't get her very far.

But was she really going to try to be hired as Angelos Mena's daughter's *nanny*?

'I'll go get her,' he said in a clipped voice, and as he strode out of the room Talia sank into one of the chairs in front of the desk. Her knees were shaking and her head throbbed. Getting this far had taken all of her physical and mental resources. Nine hours in a plane, sweating and shaking the whole time, and then wandering through the crowded streets of Athens, flinching every time someone so much as jostled her shoulder, fighting back the memories she never let herself think about, the ones that could bring bile to her throat and send her heart rate crashing in panic.

It had been utterly exhausting. And yet... Talia rose from the chair and went to the huge window that overlooked the city. In the distance she could see the crumbling ruins of the ancient Acropolis underneath a hard blue sky, and the sight was powerful enough to make her feel a flicker of awe, a lick of excitement. For a second she could remember how it had felt to be eighteen years old and full of hope and vigour, the whole world stretched out in front of her, shimmering with promise, everything an enticing adventure...

'Miss Di Sione?'

Talia whirled around, flushing guiltily at the look of disapproval on Angelos Mena's face. Should she not have looked out the window? Goodness but the man was tightly wired.

'This is Sofia.'

'Yes, of course.' Talia stepped towards the slight girl who blinked owlishly from behind her glasses. Her dark, curly hair framed a lovely, heart-shaped face; most of her right cheek was covered in the puckered red flesh of a scar. While waiting outside Talia had noticed how the girl would let her hair fall in front of her face to hide it, and her heart had twisted with sympathy. She knew what it was like to have scars. It just happened that hers were invisible.

'Hello, Sofia,' she said now, smiling, and just as before the girl bent her head forward so her hair slid in front of her face. Angelos frowned.

No, actually, he glowered. Talia quelled at the scowl on his face, and she could only wonder what his daughter felt. She'd watched Sofia covertly as she'd waited to see Angelos; she'd seen how the girl's gaze followed each woman into the office, and then how her shoulders had slumped when each woman had come out again, usually looking annoyed or embarrassed or both. A couple of times Sofia had been ushered in, and Talia had watched how her slight body had trembled and she'd gripped her hands together, her knuckles showing bony and white, as she'd stepped into that inner sanctum.

After about an hour of waiting, Talia had tried to befriend her. She'd shown her the pad of paper and pack of coloured pencils she always kept in her bag, and for fun she'd done a quick sketch of one of the women who had been waiting, exaggerating her face so she was a caricature, but still recognisable. When Sofia had recognised the woman with her beaky nose and protuberant eyes, hands like claws planted on bony hips, she'd let out a little giggle, and then clapped her hand over her mouth, her eyes wide and panicked.

Talia had grinned at her, reassuring and conspiratorial, and slowly Sofia had relaxed, dropping her hand and then pushing the pad of paper towards Talia, silently inviting her to draw another sketch. And so she had.

They'd whiled away a pleasant hour with Talia doing sketches of as many of the women as she could remember before she'd handed the pencils to Sofia and encouraged her to draw something.

Sofia had sketched a sunset, a stretch of golden sand and a wash of blue water.

'Lovely,' Talia had murmured.

'*Spiti,*' she'd said, and when Talia had looked blank, she'd translated hesitantly, 'Home.'

'Sofia?' Angelos said now, his tone sharpening. He rested a hand on his daughter's shoulder, gentle yet heavy, and spoke in Greek to her.

Sofia looked up, smiling shyly. *'Yassou.'*

Angelos spoke again in Greek and then glanced pointedly at Talia. 'I am telling my daughter that you do not know Greek.'

'Don't worry,' Talia replied lightly. 'She already knows. We've been miming for most of the afternoon, but we've managed to get along. And Sofia knows more English than you think, Mr Mena.'

'Kyrie Mena,' he corrected, and she nodded, only just keeping from rolling her eyes.

'Kyrie,' she agreed, and she didn't need Angelos Mena's wince to know she'd butchered the pronunciation.

Angelos spoke again in Greek to Sofia, and his daughter said something back in reply. Although Talia didn't know what either of them was saying, she could feel both Angelos's disapproval and Sofia's anxiety. She stood there, trying to smile even as exhaustion crashed over her again.

What was she doing here, really? She'd come all this way to find her grandfather's precious book, not interview for a nanny position. If she had any sense she'd stop this farce before it went any further, and explain to Angelos Mena the real reason why she'd come.

And then, no doubt, have him boot her out the door, and any chance to recover Giovanni's book would be gone for ever.

Angelos was talking to Sofia again in Greek and Talia could feel her vision blur as the headache that had been skirting the fringes of her mind threatened to take over. The room felt hot, the air stale, and her legs were starting to tremble again.

'Do you mind…' she murmured, and sank into the chair, dropping her head into her hands as she took several deep breaths.

Angelos broke off his conversation with his daughter to enquire sharply, 'Miss Di Sione? Are you all right?'

Talia took another deep breath as her vision started to swim.

'Miss Di Sione?'

'Talia,' she corrected him. 'And no, actually, I think I'm going to faint.'

# CHAPTER TWO

ANGELOS SWORE UNDER his breath as the woman in front of him went limp, her head drooping down between her knees.

He shouted for Eleni and then went over to Talia, crouching down by her chair as he put an arm around her shoulders and attempted to prop her up.

'Sorry,' she managed as her head lolled against his arm. She felt like a rag doll in his arms, boneless and light. Her hair brushed his cheek.

'Papa, is she going to be all right?' Sofia asked anxiously, and Angelos nearly swore again. The last thing his daughter needed was to worry about some stranger.

'Yes, of course,' he said, more tersely than he intended. 'She's just come over faint for a moment.'

His assistant came hurrying into the room, and Angelos barked out an order for a glass of water. 'Make it juice,' he snapped as Eleni headed out to the reception area. 'Her blood sugar might be low.'

He glanced back at Talia, whose eyes were closed, her once rosy face now pale and bloodless. Her golden lashes fanned her cheeks and her lips parted slightly on a shaky breath. Then her eyes fluttered open and her gaze clashed with Angelos's. For a second he felt jarred, as if he'd missed the last step on a staircase. He was suddenly conscious of his arm around her shoulders, her breasts pressed against his chest. Then she struggled to sit upright and he let his arm fall away.

'I'm so sorry,' she murmured. 'I don't normally do that.'

'Don't you?' he bit out, and she glanced at him uncertainly.

'No...'

'The thing is,' Angelos said, his voice still hard, 'I don't know the first thing about you, Miss Di Sione. And yet you want me to entrust my daughter into your care.'

She gazed at him for a moment, the hazel of her eyes so clear he felt a sudden flicker of shame at his curt tone and implied accusation. Then she looked away from him, to Sofia.

'I'm all right, Sofia,' she said softly, and Angelos saw his daughter's expression brighten as she gave Talia a trembling smile.

She was the first woman today, Angelos acknowledged, who had actually cared what his daughter was feeling. Had concerned herself with Sofia at all. And he realised that from the moment Sofia had entered his office, Talia had not made anything of his daughter's scarred face. She hadn't overcompensated either way; she'd simply acted as if it hadn't mattered at all. The realisation made him feel both glad and completely wrong-footed, because it was still obvious to him that Talia Di Sione was utterly unsuitable to be a nanny. No qualifications, no references... he didn't even know how she'd heard of the job or why she'd shown up for it.

And yet he felt on a gut level that she was the right choice, the only choice. Because she cared about his daughter.

Eleni came in with a crystal glass of apple juice on a tray and Talia took it with a murmured thanks. 'I'm sorry to be a bother,' she said, glancing at Angelos from under her lashes as she took a sip of juice. 'I'm fine now, really.'

'It's no bother.' Angelos paused. Talia was clearly the best choice for the position, and yet still he resisted. He liked things to be clear-cut, to make sense. He appreciated quantitative qualifications, experience over instinct. God knows his instincts had been wrong in the past. He trusted facts now, hard and solid and certain. Emotion, instinctual or otherwise, had no place in his life.

And yet… He watched as Talia smiled at Sofia and said something that made his daughter smile shyly back. Sofia caught his frowning gaze and gave him a hesitant smile and a discreet thumbs-up. This was the first woman she'd approved of. Should he trust his daughter's instinct as well as his own?

His resolve hardened along with the set of his jaw. He had no choice. He needed to hire a nanny today, so he could return to work and Sofia could be cared for. He turned to Talia. 'Can you be ready to leave in an hour?'

Talia blinked, her vision starting to swim again as she took in Angelos's request. *'Leave…?'* she repeated, and he gave an impatient nod.

'I'd like to return to Kallos within the hour.'

Knowing she was sounding stupid, Talia couldn't keep herself from repeating him yet again. 'Kallos…?'

'My home,' Angelos clarified. 'Did you not read the advertisement I placed, Miss Di Sione?'

*'Spiti,'* Talia said, remembering Sofia's drawing, and surprise flickered in Angelos's mahogany eyes.

'Yes, home.' He paused, his gaze sweeping over her in a way that made goose bumps rise on Talia's arms. 'So you do know a little Greek.'

'Very little.' Talia dragged a deep breath into her lungs

and tried to force her mind to clear. She felt a hot tide of embarrassment wash over her to think how weak and helpless she must have looked to Angelos Mena, practically collapsing in his office. It was just that she hadn't eaten anything for hours, and the emotional and physical exhaustion of dealing with so many strange things had finally overwhelmed her. But she was better now. She'd make herself be.

She straightened, putting the glass of juice on the desk with a clink. 'Mr—Kyrie Mena, I'm afraid this has all got a little out of hand…' She felt another blush rising as Angelos's eyebrows snapped together in irritated confusion. If she told him the real reason for her being here now, he'd be utterly furious. She might have only met the man a few minutes ago, but she knew him well enough to understand that Angelos Mena would be enraged to learn she actually had no intention or interest in being his daughter's nanny.

Except…could she really say that? Talia's gaze slid to Sofia, who was watching her anxiously, her dark hair swinging in front of her face to hide her scarred cheek. Sofia met her gaze and gave a fragile smile.

'*Parakalo,*' she whispered, which Talia knew meant *please.* 'Come,' she added, her voice tentative, the English word sounding hesitant on her lips.

Talia's heart twisted hard in sympathy, just as it had when she'd first laid eyes on this girl. Sofia wanted her to come, and it was only for six weeks. And surely in six weeks she'd find an opportunity to ask Angelos about the book, even to get him to give her the book. More importantly, she might be able to help Sofia. At least she could offer her friendship.

Why shouldn't she accept this job?

Because it was strange and unexpected, and she'd have to deal with all sorts of things she'd avoided for the last

seven years. Because she was in no position to help anyone, when she hadn't been able to help herself. When she
was already out of her depth, suffering panic attacks,
afraid of the future.

And never mind her own deficiencies, by accepting
this job she'd be deceiving this family, even if it was out
of good intentions. She was pretty sure Angelos Mena
would see her actions as questionable, perhaps even rep-
rehensible. She was no nanny.

'I...' she began, helplessly, because she had no idea
what to do. Sofia was gazing at her with puppy dog eyes
and Angelos Mena was clearly seething with impatience.
How could she refuse? How could she not?

'You did come here to apply for the position, didn't
you, Miss Di Sione?' Angelos demanded. 'I am now *offer-
ing* you the position. Are you prepared to take it or not?'

Still Talia hesitated, caught by Sofia's silently imploring look. She turned back to Angelos, whose gaze was
narrowed, everything about his powerful form exuding
impatience and irritation. 'Yes,' she said, the word catching in her throat. She cleared her throat, and then lifted
her chin. 'I am.'

The words seemed to set everything in motion, and the
next hour was a blur as Angelos barked out orders to his
assistant and Talia was shunted back to the reception area
with Sofia. She got out her pad and pencils while people
bustled around them, and she and Sofia took turns drawing funny pictures, laughing softly together, until Angelos stood before them, hands on trim hips, his dark and
commanding gaze fastened on Talia in a way that made
every thought evaporate from her brain.

'Where are your things, Miss Di Sione?'

'Um, back at the hotel where I checked in.'

'And that is?'

'Near the Acropolis…'

Angelos let out a sigh, no more than a hiss of breath. 'The name of the hotel, please?'

'The Adriana,' Talia recalled, wishing she could act a bit more with it in front of Angelos Mena. She'd dealt with plenty of rich and powerful people through her work as a portrait artist, but no one had reduced her to insensible babbling the way Angelos Mena did with his narrowed gaze and overwhelming presence, not to mention his obvious annoyance. He clearly did not suffer fools gladly, and from the moment she'd entered his impressive office she'd felt like a fool.

'I'll arrange for someone to collect your bags,' Angelos said. 'In the meantime you can wait here with Sofia.' He strode away without waiting for her reply, and Talia watched him leave. He had not even looked at his daughter, much less spared her a kind word or a smile.

She glanced at Sofia, wondering how they were going to overcome the language barrier for the next six weeks. 'Perhaps you should teach me some Greek,' she suggested, and Sofia's forehead furrowed. *'Elinika,'* she tried, fishing for the few phrases of Greek she'd learned on the plane trip over here. She touched her mouth to indicate speaking, and Sofia brightened.

*'Ne, ne.'* She pointed to her chest. 'Speak *Anglika.'*

Talia nodded, smiling in understanding. 'We can teach each other.'

They spent the next hour teaching each other words and phrases in both English and Greek, amidst much laughter when one of them, usually Talia, got it wrong.

'Gi-neck-a,' Talia repeated after Sofia. 'Now what is that?' Laughing, Sofia pointed to her. 'Nanny?' Talia guessed. 'American? Foreigner?'

'Woman,' Angelos said quietly, and everything in Talia

jolted as she turned to look at him. He was standing in front of them, gazing at her with an inscrutable expression, which was better than his usual scowl, although it still made Talia feel uncertain. *'Gyneka,'* he added, making Talia realise she'd butchered the pronunciation once again. 'Woman.' For a second, no more, his gaze remained on Talia; she felt as if he'd pinned her there, so she was unable to look away, or even to breathe.

Then he flicked his gaze away, towards his daughter. Talia couldn't understand the Greek but the quick jerk of his head towards the elevator conveyed his meaning well enough. It was time to go.

She slipped the pad and pencils back into her bag and stood with Sofia. Angelos turned back to her.

'The helicopter is ready, and your things have been fetched from the hotel.'

'Helicopter…' She stared at him in alarm. 'You didn't say anything about a helicopter.'

Angelos frowned. 'How else would we get to Kallos?'

'By car?' she guessed hopefully, and Angelos's nostrils flared.

'Kallos is an island, Miss Di Sione. We will travel there by helicopter. It should only take an hour.'

An island. She thought of Sofia's drawing, the blue water, the beach. Of course it was an island.

She realised she must have been gaping at him because Angelos's lips compressed as he looked at her. 'Is that a problem?' he asked, his tone deceptively mild.

'No, of course not.' But she was lying, because she could already feel the panic starting its insistent staccato pulse inside her. What on earth was she doing, going goodness knew where with this stranger? In a *helicopter*?

Her breath hitched and Angelos glanced at her. 'You aren't going to faint again?'

'No,' Talia said with far more certainty than she felt. In the past twenty-four hours she'd gone about five thousand miles outside her comfort zone. She wasn't sure she could manage another step.

Then she felt a small, cold hand slide into hers and she looked down to see Sofia smiling at her. 'Okay?' she asked, and Talia was touched and humbled by the girl's obvious concern.

'Okay,' she confirmed shakily, and hand in hand they walked towards the lift.

Even with Sofia's support Talia couldn't keep the fear from kicking up her heart rate as they took the lift up to the top of the building where a helicopter was waiting on a helipad.

She glanced at Angelos, who was striding towards the machine, the wind from the whirring propellers moulding his shirt and suit jacket close to his body so Talia could see the impressive outline of his well-defined pecs. The helicopter looked small and menacing, its curved windshield looking like the giant eyes of a bug. Talia clutched Sofia's hand harder.

She really didn't think she could do this.

Angelos climbed into the helicopter, and then reached down first for Sofia's hand. Talia watched as the little girl clambered easily inside and then sat down. Angelos turned back to her, the wind whipping about him, his hand outstretched. Talia simply stared.

'Miss Di Sione,' he shouted over the noise of the propeller blades. 'Take my hand.'

Talia's heart was pounding painfully, and her palms were icy and damp with sweat. She couldn't do this. She couldn't deal with confined spaces, ones where it was impossible to get out. A closed door, a dark room, a locked car…she avoided them all. And the passenger jet she'd been on a few hours ago had been hard enough, but a *helicopter*...

And then suddenly she thought of Giovanni smiling at her as he'd given her his instructions. *'I know you will try your hardest. And you will succeed.'*

Taking a deep breath, she reached for Angelos's hand and then she let him pull her up into the helicopter. She practically collapsed into her seat, her legs rubbery and her heart thudding sickly. She had just managed to jam her seat belt together when the helicopter lifted off the building and began its ascent into a cloudless blue sky, heading for the Aegean Sea.

# CHAPTER THREE

ANGELOS STUDIED HIS new nanny, noting dispassionately how pale she'd gone, her eyes closed as she leaned back against the seat and took several deep, even breaths. What on earth was the woman's problem?

'Do you suffer from travel sickness?' he asked abruptly, raising his voice to be heard above the noise of the helicopter, and her eyes flew open.

'No.'

'Then why do you look so terrible?'

'You're quite the flatterer, aren't you,' she muttered, and Angelos stared at her, nonplussed.

'You look as if you are about to be sick.'

'You'd better hope I'm not,' Talia answered, and he grimaced in distaste.

'Indeed, I do. It would make for a most unpleasant journey.'

'That it would.' Talia let out a shuddering breath as she shifted in her seat. 'And it's already pretty awful.'

'You do not like helicopters.'

'No.' She'd closed her eyes again, her face scrunched up, and Angelos inspected her for another moment. Her hair was going curly in the heat and he could see a sprinkling of golden freckles across her nose. He wondered how old she was, and realised afresh how little he knew about her besides her name. What on earth had possessed him to hire her?

Talia opened her eyes and turned to Sofia. 'You don't mind helicopters,' she remarked, and with a bit of play-acting, miming the propeller blades and making a face, she communicated her meaning.

Sofia grinned. 'Home,' she said in English. 'I like home.'

'I like home too,' Talia said with a sigh. 'But I'm sure I'll like yours as well.' Sofia wrinkled her nose, not understanding, and Talia leaned over and patted her hand before she sank back against the seat and closed her eyes.

Angelos continued to study her for a moment, wondering how she'd ended up in his office. How had she even heard of the advertisement, and why had she come without a CV? Questions, he decided, he would not ask her in the noisy confines of the helicopter, with Sofia trying to catch every word. He would have time to discover just who his new nanny was later, and make sure she was an appropriate companion for his daughter.

His gaze moved to Sofia; she was leaning towards the window, watching the sea slide by. She never liked leaving the safety of Kallos, and she seemed to shrink even more into herself whenever he took her to Athens. He knew people stared at her scarred face, and the attention made Sofia embarrassed and exceedingly shy. He was grateful that Talia Di Sione, for all her idiosyncrasies, had not once made Sofia feel ashamed of her scar.

'Look, Papa,' Sofia called in Greek, and he leaned forward to see a sleek white sailboat cutting through the blue-green waters.

'Beautiful,' he murmured, and then glanced back at Talia. She still had her eyes closed. Impulsively he reached over and touched her shoulder. Her eyes flew open and she jerked upright as if he'd branded her with a hot poker.

'Relax,' he said. 'I just thought you might appreciate the view.'

'I'd rather just get onto land,' Talia muttered, but she obligingly looked out the window of the helicopter, and Angelos watched as her face softened into a smile as she took in the stunning vista of sea and sky.

'I always wanted to see the Greek islands,' she said.

'You have not been here before?'

'No, this was my first time in Athens.'

'How long had you been in the city?'

She shot him a wry look. 'About six hours.'

'Six hours?' Angelos frowned. 'Do you mean you arrived in Athens *today*?' She nodded. 'But what on earth made you apply for the job, having just arrived?'

She looked away, seeming uneasy. Suspicion hardened inside him. What was going on with this woman? 'It seemed like a good idea,' she said at last.

Angelos didn't answer. He could see Sofia looking at them both and he had no intention of pursuing an uncomfortable line of enquiry with Talia Di Sione when his daughter was present. But he *would* get to the bottom of why she was here.

Fifteen minutes later the helicopter began to make its descent to Kallos. As soon as they'd landed Angelos clambered out of the helicopter, and then reached back a hand for Sofia and then Talia.

He was conscious of how small and slender her hand felt in his as she stepped down onto the rocky earth, shading her eyes with her other hand as she gazed round the island.

'Is this a private island?' she asked.

'Yes, it is my home. But you will have everything you need. The villa is well supplied by nearby Naxos.'

She nodded slowly, letting out a breath she must have been holding for a while. 'Okay,' she said, and she sounded as if she were talking to herself. 'Okay.'

Angelos led the way from the helipad to the villa. The salt-tinged sea breeze buffeted him and the sun was hot above and for a moment he breathed in the air and let himself relax. Let himself believe that he had things under control, that Sofia was safe.

That he'd done the best he could, even when he hadn't before.

Talia took several deep breaths of fresh sea air as she followed Angelos and Sofia down the winding path to the sprawling whitewashed villa by the beach. The tension that had been throbbing in her temples since she'd stepped into the helicopter was finally starting to ease.

From the vantage point of the helipad she'd been able to see how small the island was: a large villa with extensive gardens, a staff cottage and a stony, hilly rise to a beach on the other side. *Small.* But small could be good, she told herself. She didn't have to feel claustrophobic here. She wasn't in a closed space, with the open air and sea all around her, and at least she wouldn't have to deal with a lot of strange people.

Still she felt tense. She felt like sprinting back to the safety of her grandfather's estate, the quiet studio with its views of sea and sky, where she could paint in blissful solitude. Where she didn't have to come up hard against all her old fears and insecurities.

She took a deep breath and tilted her face to the sun. She could do this. She *was* doing this. She'd survived a plane trip, a taxi ride through a heaving city, a helicopter ride and near constant interactions with strangers. It was more than she'd had to deal with in seven years, and it had exhausted her, but she'd survived.

'Are you all right?' Angelos called, and Talia realised she'd stopped walking, and had dropped behind Angelos and Sofia.

'I'm fine,' she said, and hurried down the path to join her employer and his daughter.

As they came into the villa, the rooms airy and spacious and light, a housekeeper bustled up to them, exclaiming in Greek as she kissed Sofia on both cheeks. Then she stopped in front of Talia and, planting her hands on ample hips, gave her a thorough once-over with narrowed eyes. She spoke to Angelos, who answered in Greek. Talia had no idea what they were saying, but she suspected she'd come up wanting in the housekeeper's well-trained eye.

'Do I pass?' she asked Angelos when there was a break in the conversation. She'd meant to sound teasing but it came out anxious instead. Tension knotted her stomach muscles again as she realised afresh how *strange* this all was. And she really didn't like strange.

Angelos looked startled, and then his mouth compressed in a way she was already finding familiar. 'My housekeeper's opinion is of no concern. I have already hired you.'

'It's that bad, huh?' Talia only half joked. At least this time she sounded light, even if she didn't feel it. 'I know my dress is wrinkled, but I *have* been on a plane.'

He inclined his head towards the stairs. 'Maria will show you your room. You will have time to refresh yourself and dress appropriately before dinner.'

The man had no sense of humour, Talia decided as she followed Maria up the stairs. No sense of compassion or friendliness or sensitivity. He was a machine. A robot. A drone...

She was so busy thinking she almost slammed into Maria's substantial form as the housekeeper stopped in the doorway of a bedroom.

'Your room,' she said in heavily accented English, and Talia peeked around her to see a gorgeous room decorated in sea-green and cream, the louvered shutters of the windows open to the beach.

'It's lovely,' she said. *'Efharisto.'* Maria grunted her grudging approval at Talia's passable Greek, and then with her fingers mimed seven o'clock. 'Dinner at seven?' Talia guessed, and as the housekeeper nodded and left she wondered if she could take a crash course in Greek.

She moved to the windows, taking in the spectacular sight. Gardens bursting with bougainvillea and heliotrope ran down a sloping hill to the beach, a stretch of white sand that met up with the blue-green water, just like in Sofia's picture.

The housekeeper had directed Sofia to the kitchen as soon as they arrived, and judging from the tantalising baking smells coming from that direction, Talia had suspected there was a snack in store. Her own stomach growled at the thought and she checked her watch. Two hours until dinner. Time, hopefully, to make herself presentable, although she had a feeling Angelos Mena would judge her wanting no matter what she wore or how much effort she took with her appearance. But at least he'd hired her.

Still Talia relished a soak in the huge marble tub, washing away the grime of nearly twenty-four hours of travel and reviving her tired spirits. She unpacked her single suitcase, realising belatedly that she had not brought nearly enough for six weeks. In fact, she'd packed nothing but serviceable T-shirts and shorts, a single fleece and a pair of jeans, and the crumpled sundress she'd worn on the plane.

Biting her lip, Talia acknowledged she had nothing remotely *appropriate* to wear for dinner that night. In her normal life she never needed to dress to impress, and her career as an artist meant work wear was usually paint-splattered jeans and old T-shirts. She hadn't even considered bringing something businesslike to wear for her meeting with Angelos Mena; in truth, she hadn't thought much beyond surviving the journey. She hadn't had the heart or head space for more.

Sighing, she wondered if she had time to wash her sundress and let it dry in the sea breeze.

She discovered that she *almost* had time, when she headed out of her bedroom at five to seven, the dress clean and far less wrinkled, but slightly damp across the shoulders. Hopefully Angelos wouldn't notice.

The villa was quiet as Talia came down the stairs, the rooms darkened and empty. She peeked into an enormous living room scattered with linen sofas in natural shades, and then a masculine-looking study with a huge mahogany desk and book-lined walls. Finally she found the dining room towards the back of the house; Angelos was already standing in the room, gazing up at a large portrait of a woman hanging on the far wall.

He turned as Talia tiptoed in, his face snapping into its usual frown. 'You're late.'

'I'm sorry. I was looking for the dining room.'

His frown deepened as he took in her outfit. 'You have not changed.'

'Actually, I have. I washed my dress and put it back on.' For some reason that made her blush, and to cover it she did a ridiculous little twirl. 'Can't you tell?' She stopped, her dress swishing around her legs, and saw that Angelos's frown had morphed into a positive scowl, grooves visible from nose to mouth, eyes dangerously narrowed.

Even scowling, the man was devastatingly attractive.

He'd changed his grey business suit for a crisp white shirt, open at the throat, and dark trousers. The clothes were basic and should have been boring, but on his powerful frame the white cotton drew Talia's attention to his broad shoulders, the dark trousers to his trim hips and powerful thighs.

Appalled by her perusal, she yanked her gaze away from his muscular form. She'd been looking at his *thighs*, for heaven's sake. Hopefully he hadn't noticed her moment of shameless goggling.

Now she saw the plush velvet chairs and huge polished table set for two. 'Is Sofia not joining us?'

'You *washed* your dress?' Angelos sounded incredulous and Talia lifted her chin.

'I'm sorry, I didn't realise I'd be required to wear an evening gown.' She walked to the place setting at one end of the table, resting her hand on the back of the chair. 'Where's Sofia?'

'She's eating with Maria.'

'Is that what usually happens?' Talia watched as Angelos walked around the table to pull out her chair.

'In future, you may dine with her if you wish, but tonight I wanted to speak to you alone.'

'Oh.' Since he was holding out her chair Talia sat down. She breathed in the woodsy scent of his aftershave as he pushed her chair in; his face was close to hers, close enough to make goose bumps rise on her arms, and she suppressed the urge to shiver. She wondered what his jaw would feel like, if his clean-shaven face would be smooth, or possess a hint of roughness. Like the man himself, urbanity not quite cloaking a cold, ruthless interior.

Angelos walked smoothly around the table and sat down at the opposite end, placing his napkin in his lap with a brisk flourish. Talia did the same. Although she lived in a house that more than rivalled Angelos Mena's in terms of space and sheer luxury, she still felt awed by his home and his presence. Back on Giovanni's estate, she took most meals in the kitchen or in her studio while she was working. When she ate with Giovanni, they had a quiet meal listening to the radio or watching TV. She hadn't been to a dinner party since…well, she couldn't even remember since when. A Christmas or Thanksgiving meal with her brothers and sisters hadn't felt as ornate or intimidating as a meal alone with this man.

Maria came in with the first course, a salad of plump tomatoes and slices of cucumber sprinkled with feta cheese. 'This is very civilised,' Talia said when the housekeeper had left. 'Thank you.'

'May I never be accused of being uncivilised,' Angelos responded dryly.

Talia watched him covertly as she ate her salad, wondering at this man who, if her research was correct, possessed a priceless volume of poetry and had bid on a second by the same anonymous poet. That was how she'd tracked him down; she'd found an obscure website with a message board where people could post the rare books they were looking for. She'd stumbled across a message posted by an agent acting on Angelos's behalf, or at least on the behalf of Mena Consultancy. She just hoped it meant that Angelos actually had the book.

What if after everything she'd endured and agreed to, this was nothing more than a wild goose chase?

'So do you and Sofia live on Kallos all year long?' she asked.

'Sofia does. I travel for work. In fact, I have to leave tomorrow.'

So he wouldn't be here for the six weeks of her stay? Talia felt a wave of relief at the thought, as well as a twinge of disappointment for Sofia. No matter how stern or auto-cratic Angelos seemed, it couldn't be good for him to be away from his daughter so much.

'Isn't it rather lonely here for a girl her age?' she asked.

'Sofia prefers it. She has a tutor who comes in by boat for her lessons, and Maria and the other staff for company. And, of course, now you.'

'Has she had other nannies?'

'Yes, but I'm afraid none of them have lasted very long.' Angelos's voice was clipped, his gaze shuttered. 'I hope this next one will be a better fit.'

'Why haven't they lasted very long?' Talia asked, cu-rious. Sofia didn't seem like a difficult child, and the set-ting was practically paradise. Surely it was a dream job for anyone looking for a position in child care.

Angelos shrugged. 'They did not find the situation to their liking. But you are asking all the questions, Miss Di Sione, and I invited you to dinner so *I* could ask the questions.'

'And here I thought we were just having a conversation,' Talia answered lightly, but Angelos did not give so much as a flicker of a smile. She speared a cucumber. 'Ask away, then,' she said with an insouciance she didn't remotely feel. She didn't want Angelos Mena asking her probing questions, at least not yet. She had no idea how to answer anything. She hated the thought of lying, but total hon-esty felt impossible at this point. 'But first,' she added, 'I must ask one last thing, and that is that you call me Talia.'

She popped the cucumber in her mouth only to have it stick in her throat as Angelos answered, an edge to his smooth voice, 'Very well, *Talia*. I want to ask you just why you came to Athens, and more to the point, to my *of-fice*, since it obviously wasn't to seek a position as nanny.'

# CHAPTER FOUR

WITH THE CUCUMBER stuck in her throat, Talia erupted into an inelegant fit of coughing. Angelos poured her a glass of water and pushed it across the table, watching unsympathetically all the while.

Talia took a few sips, thankful that she'd managed at least to stop coughing. 'Sorry about that,' she said on a gasp.

'You haven't answered my question.' Angelos's gaze was narrowed, his lips compressed, his arms folded. He wasn't exuding warm fuzzies—that was for sure.

Talia took another forkful of salad in order to give her time to think of a reply. How much to admit? She felt instinctively that if she were to talk about her true reason for coming to Greece now, Angelos would have her back on that helicopter so quick her head would be spinning as fast as the propeller blades.

And the truth was, she didn't want to leave. Not just because she needed to find her grandfather's book, but for Sofia's sake as well. Already she was forming a picture of what the little girl's life here on Kallos had to be like, lonely and isolated, with only a few elderly staff for company.

*Kind of like yours, then.*

The realisation gave her an uncomfortable jolt. She didn't think of herself as either lonely or isolated, not with her work for stimulation and her grandfather for company. Perhaps Sofia was happy here, just as she was happy on her grandfather's estate. Maybe she wasn't as needed as she'd felt she was…which still left her with no idea how to answer Angelos's question.

'Talia? I am waiting.'

Talia jerked her unfocused gaze back to Angelos. He'd laid down his fork and put his hands flat on the table, his dark gaze fastened on hers, hard and unyielding. The man looked seriously annoyed, but even with the irritation flashing in his whisky-brown eyes Talia couldn't keep from noticing the lean planes of his cheek and jaw, the warm olive tone of his skin. If he'd just smile a bit more, she might start seriously crushing on him.

But considering their situation, it was probably better that he didn't smile.

'You're right that I wasn't looking to be a nanny,' Talia said finally, choosing her words with care. 'I came to Athens for a…a different reason. But when you assumed I was there for the nanny position, it seemed…fortuitous that I apply. And accept.' That much was true at least.

'Fortuitous,' Angelos repeated flatly. 'How so?'

'I like Sofia, Mr—Kyrie Mena. She seems a very kind girl. I want to help her, or at least be her friend.'

'And yet with, by your own admission, absolutely no child-care experience, you think you have the ability, even the expertise, to help her?'

Talia blinked at his scathing tone. 'I may not have child-care experience, but I know what it is like to be a child—'

'As does every person on this planet.'

'I know what it's like to be lonely,' she burst out, and then wished she hadn't. She wasn't lonely. She'd always told Giovanni she wasn't, and she'd believed herself. She *had*.

'My daughter is not lonely,' Angelos informed her shortly. 'She has everything she needs here on Kallos.'

'Everything?' Exasperated, Talia shook her head. 'Then why did you hire me?'

'I'm asking myself that question as well,' he retorted. He sat back, taking a measured breath. Talia could feel the crackle of tension in the air. 'The truth is,' he continued, 'I was running out of both time and options. And,' he conceded grudgingly, 'Sofia seems to have formed some kind of attachment to you. But I must confess, in our short acquaintance, you have not recommended yourself to me, Miss Di Sione.'

'Talia.'

'*Talia*. You have in fact seemed extraordinarily short-sighted and, dare I say it, flighty—'

'I think you just dared,' Talia snapped before she could think better of it. She felt annoyed and bizarrely hurt by his quick and brutal judgement. What did Angelos Mena know about her, really? Only that she hadn't packed very much and she didn't do well in helicopters. And for that he felt capable of dismissing her as a person?

'You disagree with me?' he enquired, and she let out a huff of disbelieving laughter. No doubt Angelos Mena expected her to bow and scrape and apologise—and for what? Coming over a little dizzy?

'Of course I do. You don't know me, Kyrie Mena. You didn't know I existed until a couple of hours ago. How can you say I'm anything when you've barely met me?'

'I am basing my opinions on what I've seen so far. I'm a consultant, Miss—'

'Talia.'

'Talia.' He expelled her name on a hiss of breath. 'It's my job to come into a situation and assess it swiftly.'

'Too swiftly, maybe. What are you basing your judgement on? That I didn't pack more than one dress or that I was a little nervous in your helicopter?' She raised her eyebrows in challenge, half amazed at her own daring. She didn't normally pick a fight, but then she didn't normally need to. She'd cocooned herself in safety and isolation instead. It felt kind of good to come out swinging. Strangely empowering. She'd much rather stand tall than shrink back. 'Well?' she challenged when he didn't answer. 'Which is it?'

Angelos leaned back in his chair. 'I take your point,' he said after a pause. His face was expressionless, his gaze implacable. Of course it would be too much to expect to see a glimmer of apology in those darkly glowing eyes. 'But surely you can understand my concern,' he continued. 'I am entrusting my daughter, my only child, to your care.'

'Of course I can understand your concern.' Talia sighed, the fight going out of her. 'If I had a daughter, I'd feel the same.' Angelos had hired her without knowing anything about her. He had the right to ask some questions, to be a bit sceptical. And she was hiding something, just as he suspected. Perhaps if she admitted her interest in the book...but no. She needed him to get to know her first. 'If you'd like to know more about me,' she said, trying to smile, 'then all you have to do is ask.'

He studied her for a moment, his gaze assessing and speculative. Talia suppressed the urge to squirm or fidget under his unnervingly direct and unblinking stare. 'You're American,' he said at last, and she gave a shaky breath of relief at the innocuousness of that statement.

'Yes.'

'Where do you come from?'

'Outside New York City.'

He nodded slowly. 'You must be in your mid-twenties. You had a job before this?'

'Yes, and I still have it. I'm an artist.'

'An artist,' he repeated, sounding decidedly unimpressed. He spoke as if she dabbled in finger paints in her free time.

'A portrait artist,' Talia clarified. 'I work on commissions.'

'I see.'

What he saw, Talia suspected, was that she was an unemployed airhead who traipsed around the world, being short-sighted and flighty. It was foolish of her to be so rankled, so hurt, by his assessment, and yet she was. No one had ever sized her up and dismissed her so thoroughly before. She'd worked hard for her reputation as a reclusive but talented artist. She hated the thought that Angelos was judging her, and so harshly at that.

'You said you wished to help my daughter,' Angelos said after a pause. Again with that direct stare, and Talia forced herself not to look away, to find some way to hide from Angelos Mena's searching gaze and questions. Being the focus of his full attention felt like standing on a beach, watching as a tidal wave gained in towering power, readying to crash down on you. 'How do you think you could help her?' he pressed.

'By being her friend,' Talia answered.

His gaze blazed into hers. 'I am not paying you to be her friend.'

'Very well,' Talia answered, trying not to quake under that unyielding stare, 'perhaps you should tell me what you're paying me for exactly. You haven't actually told me what my duties are.' Angelos had the grace to look slightly discomfited, his gaze thankfully flicking away from hers for a second, giving Talia the courage to add, 'Not to mention an actual job contract or reference check or any of the usual protocols. I mean,' she continued as she shrugged expansively, 'if you want to talk about being short-sighted or, I don't know, *flighty*.'

Angelos turned back to her, his lips tightening, his nostrils flared with annoyance, and Talia wondered if she'd gone too far. She didn't actually want to be fired. She certainly didn't want to get in that helicopter again anytime soon. But she hadn't been able to resist pushing back just a little. If Angelos Mena was a different kind of man, he might have even smiled at her pointed joke.

For one tantalising second she imagined that granite gaze softening, those sensual lips curving into an answering smile, that hard body relaxing towards her, and she felt a weird leaping sensation in her middle. She pressed one hand to her stomach to soothe those sudden butterflies. Better for him not to tease. He was so much easier to resist that way.

'Very well,' he said stiffly. 'I am happy to give you the details now. You are to be a companion to my daughter and provide her with stimulating conversation and activities when she is not at her lessons.'

'And when is she at her lessons?'

'Her tutor comes to the island every weekday morning, for a few hours until lunchtime.'

'Could she not go to a school near here?' Talia asked. 'On Naxos, maybe? To be with other children?'

'She prefers to be on the island.' Angelos's tone was final, and despite the iron warning she heard in his voice not to ask any more questions, Talia continued.

'Is that because of her scarring?' she asked quietly, and Angelos stilled.

'What about her scarring?'

'I noticed she seemed self-conscious about it,' she explained carefully. 'And it's hard for any child to feel different.'

Angelos hesitated, and in the ensuing silence Maria came in to clear the plates. Talia thanked her in clumsy Greek and the woman brusquely nodded her acceptance before turning away. Talia wondered if the housekeeper would ever thaw towards her. She'd seemed suspicious and unimpressed from the moment Talia had stepped into the villa. Someone else who'd judged her and found her wanting.

'Sofia suffered burns in a fire when she was a baby,' Angelos said abruptly. Talia opened her mouth to reply, but he cut her off before she could frame a syllable. 'It is a very painful memory for her. We do not discuss it. Ever.' He held her gaze for one long, taut moment, and Talia's mouth dried at the implacable look in his eyes. *Message received.*

Then Maria came in with the main course and Talia knew the chance, if there ever had been one, to say anything about the fire had passed. Angelos would clearly brook no more discussion of it, and she wasn't brave enough to press.

Still her mind whirled with this new information as Maria set plates of lamb souvlaki in front of them. Was it a house fire? Had Angelos been there? And what of his wife? She hadn't even given the woman a thought, and she realised she hadn't because it had been so glaringly obvious that no woman was around. She knew what a motherless home looked like, felt like. That had been another point of sympathy with Sofia, one that had been so innate Talia hadn't even realised it until now.

'Do you have any other questions?' Angelos asked. 'I will have my assistant in Athens draw up a contract and fax it to my office here. If you have any concerns while I am away, you can reach me by email, which Maria has.'

'While you're away?' Talia repeated, remembering that

he'd said he was leaving tomorrow. 'How long will you be gone?'

Angelos's mouth thinned. 'A few weeks. I can hardly work from an island in the middle of the Aegean.'

'It seems like everyone is telecommuting these days,' Talia answered. 'Can't you?'

'I'm afraid not.' He took a sip of water, effectively closing down the conversation.

Talia stared at him, wondering how close he was to Sofia. She'd sensed a yearning in the girl, a desire to please her father even as she tensed when she was around him. But what did Angelos feel for Sofia? Didn't he realise how important he was to her, especially with her mother gone? 'Won't you miss your daughter?' she asked.

He set his glass down with a firm clink. 'That is hardly your concern.'

'No, but it may be Sofia's,' Talia answered. 'Surely she'd like to spend more time with her father. Especially considering—'

'Your job,' Angelos cut across her in a hard voice, 'is to be her companion, not form an opinion on any aspect of her or my life.'

Talia nodded and swallowed down her protests. She knew she'd been terribly outspoken. She was this man's employee and she barely knew him. But she *knew* what it felt like to be without a mother or father, and she was incredibly thankful for Giovanni's care and devotion during her childhood. But Sofia didn't have a doting grandfather in her life, at least as far as Talia could tell.

'So you have no other questions,' Angelos said, a statement, and Talia merely shook her head.

They ate in tense silence for a few moments; the souvlaki was delicious but Talia barely registered a mouthful. Finally she couldn't stand the silence any longer and so she nodded towards the large portrait of a woman that hung in pride of place on the far wall.

'That is a beautiful portrait. Is it of a relative?' The portrait was of a young woman with dark hair pulled back in a loose bun, her heavy-lidded gaze full of secret amusement, her lips curved in a small, knowing smile. 'She reminds me of the *Mona Lisa*.'

Angelos didn't look at the portrait as he answered. 'It is of my late wife,' he said, and after that Talia didn't dare ask any more questions.

An hour later Angelos strode through his bedroom, shrugging out of his suit jacket and loosening his tie. Outside a silver sickle moon hung in an endless starlit sky, the sea like a smooth, dark plate underneath. Angelos braced a forearm against the window frame as he let the serene beauty of the scene wash over him.

His dinner with Talia Di Sione had left him feeling unsettled, even angry; she'd been like a stick prodding the hornet's nest of emotions he'd kept buried deep inside for the last seven years. He'd seen the judgement in her clear hazel eyes when he'd said he was leaving Sofia. He'd felt her censure at learning he would be away for several weeks.

But Talia Di Sione had no idea how it felt to gaze at his daughter every day and know it was his fault, *entirely* his fault, that she felt more comfortable hidden away on an island than living the kind of life any young girl would want, with friends and school and a mother who loved her with all of her heart.

The emotion Talia had stirred up rose within him, and resolutely, relentlessly, Angelos clamped it down. Now was not the time to indulge in self-pity, especially considering he was the last person who was deserving of any such sentiment.

He let out a long, low breath and then turned from the window. He would work; work always made him focus, helped him to forget, at least for a little while.

He moved through the villa to his study downstairs, turning on a lamp and powering up his laptop. Yet even as he reread the notes he'd made on the latest company he was helping to turn around, his mind wandered back upstairs to the woman occupying a bedroom only a few doors down from his own.

Talia Di Sione was an impossible, aggravating mystery. He had never had someone speak to him with such flippant irreverence as she had, and he found himself, to his own irritation, to feel both appalled and reluctantly admiring of her spirit. And yet she'd seemed positively terrified when they'd boarded the helicopter, and she'd practically fainted in his office. The woman was an utter contradiction, and he still knew very little about her.

He knew Maria would tell him if Talia was unsuitable in any way; she'd kept an eye on the previous nannies, most of them unfortunate young women who had taken the post in the hopes of becoming the next Kyria Mena. A few of those women Angelos had had no choice but to fire; others had left in a huff when their cringingly obvious seduction attempts had failed.

Talia, at least, didn't seem interested in him that way, if her snappy comebacks were anything to go by. Yet before he could keep himself from it, he imagined what a seduction attempt by Talia Di Sione would look like. Her hair loose and wavy about her face, her hazel eyes sparkling, her lips parted invitingly as she walked towards him, hips subtly swaying, that sundress sliding over her slight curves…

Horrified by the nature of his thoughts and his body's insistent and alarming response, Angelos quashed the provocative image immediately. He slammed the lid of his laptop down and rose from his desk, pacing the confines of his study in an attempt to keep his body under tight control. It had been a long time since he'd been with a woman, but he wasn't so desperate or deprived that he needed to fantasise about his nanny.

Shaking his head in self-disgust, he left his study and headed back upstairs. The hall was quiet, no light shining from under any of the doors. His body now firmly under control, Angelos walked past Talia's bedroom to his daughter's, quietly opening the door and slipping inside the darkened room.

Sofia was asleep in bed, her knees tucked up to her chest, one hand resting palm upwards on the pillow next to her face. Lying as she was, her scarred cheek against the pillow, she almost looked whole. Healthy in both mind and body. Angelos could almost believe she hadn't been burned, that he hadn't damaged his daughter for ever.

Gently he smoothed a tendril of curly dark hair, hair just like Xanthe's, away from her forehead. She stirred slightly, her lips pursing in a frown before her expression smoothed out and she settled back into sleep.

'S'agapo, manaria mou,' he whispered. His little lamb. With a sad smile Angelos touched his daughter's cheek and then quietly left the room.

# CHAPTER FIVE

TALIA WOKE TO sunlight streaming through the latticed shutters of her bedroom and the sound of the surf outside. Buoyed by both the light and sound, she threw off the covers and went to the window, opening the shutters wide.

The sight that greeted her was enough to make her sigh in pure pleasure. Sunlight gilded a perfect paradise: blue-green waters and soft white sand, the riot of pink and red flowers tumbling all the way to the beach. Leaning her elbows on the sill she inhaled the scents of flowers and sand and sea, the prospect and possibilities of the next six weeks filling her with something close to joy.

When had she last had an adventure or felt excitement at what the day might bring? Smiling at the thought, she reached for her smartphone to send a quick email to her grandfather.

Arrived in Greece safely. Having a surprising and wonderful time.
Love, T.

Tossing her phone on the bed, she acknowledged that she wasn't actually having a wonderful time. *Yet.* The memory of her dinner last night with Angelos and his scathing assessment of her still stung. But Angelos was leaving today, and she'd be spending most of her time with Sofia. Wonderful might be just around the corner.

She was just getting dressed in a pair of shorts and a T-shirt when the loud, insistent sound of a helicopter starting up sent her to the window again. She watched as the helicopter she'd flown in last night lifted off the helipad and like some large, ugly insect rose in the sky and began to move away.

Angelos was leaving already? It wasn't even eight in the morning. Clearly he couldn't wait to get away from Kallos, a thought that made her frown. She wondered how much time Angelos spent with his daughter, if any. And then she reminded herself, as Angelos had told her last night, that it wasn't her concern.

Dressed, her hair caught back in a practical ponytail, Talia headed downstairs. She found Maria in the kitchen, chopping vegetables for lunch. She barely glanced at Talia before nodding to the table, where two places had been set. Talia could see from one of the settings that Sofia had already eaten, and so she sat at the other and spooned yogurt and honey into a bowl.

'Sofia?' she asked the housekeeper, searching for some of the Greek phrases she'd tried to memorise. *'Apu pu iste?'* she tried, and Maria looked at her, clearly amused.

'Where am I from?'

'Oh.' Talia stared at her, nonplussed. 'You speak English.'

'A bit,' Maria answered. 'I am from Naxos.'

'Sorry, I meant where Sofia is. Currently.' Talia shook her head. 'I admit, my Greek is severely limited. But last night you seemed like you didn't speak English at all.'

'Well.' Maria let out a huff of breath. 'I wasn't sure of you.'

Talia laughed at that. 'And now you are?'

'No,' Maria answered bluntly, 'but you didn't make eyes at Kyrie Mena last night, so I am reassured that you are not trying to seduce him.'

'*Seduce...*' Talia nearly choked on her mouthful of yogurt. 'I most certainly am not. He is doing his best to terrify me though.'

Maria nodded sagely. 'That is what Kyrie Mena does. And rather well.'

'You speak more than a bit of English,' Talia exclaimed, and Maria smiled slyly.

'I'm a quick learner.'

Talia laughed again and shook her head. Somehow she seemed to have made an ally of the housekeeper, and for that she was glad. She had a feeling she would need allies. 'So...are you telling me that some of the other nannies have tried to...to seduce Kyrie Mena?'

Maria pursed her lips and then turned back to her vegetables, beheading a bunch of carrots with one swift chop. 'You could say that. If a woman crawls naked into a man's bed, it is a seduction, *ne*?'

This time Talia did choke on her yogurt. She grabbed a napkin and pressed it to her mouth, gazing at Maria in stunned disbelief. 'Not really...' she finally managed.

Maria nodded grimly. 'It is true. The woman was shown the door that night. Kyrie Mena did not even wait until morning to have her back on the mainland.' She gave Talia a quick, sideways glance. 'But I do not gossip.'

'No, of course not.' Talia took another spoonful of yogurt, her mind now full of rather salacious images of some eager nanny spread out like a centrefold, lying in wait for Angelos. And Angelos coming into his darkened bedroom, loosening his tie, unbuttoning his shirt...

Before she could stop herself she was imagining his brisk strip tease, the way he'd shrug out of a shirt, and how solid and muscular his chest would be, the moonlight casting silver shadows over his olive skin…

*Good grief.* A blush rose to Talia's face as she realised just how far she'd strayed into fantasy territory. And about Angelos Mena of all people, whom she didn't even like. He certainly had no regard for her. What on earth was she thinking?

'Sofia is upstairs,' Maria said, and Talia was grateful for the distraction. 'She is waiting for Ava, who comes for her lessons.'

Talia nodded and quickly finished her breakfast, taking her dishes to the sink before going in search of Sofia.

She still felt weirdly affected by that stupid little fantasy, as if someone might be able to guess the nature of her thoughts just from looking at her. All right, Angelos Mena was a handsome man. A very handsome man. A stunningly virile and sexy man, *fine*. And maybe she had extremely limited experience with the opposite sex. A boyfriend at seventeen, a couple of kisses. So what?

It didn't mean she had to fantasise about the first good-looking man who came into her orbit. And anyway, it wasn't as if Angelos Mena was the first good-looking man she'd ever seen. William Talbot III, whose portrait she had painted just a few months ago, was very attractive. Admittedly, he thought so too, and he'd insisted on being painted with his golf clubs and two yappy terriers, but *still*. He was, objectively speaking, a good-looking man.

But he was, Talia acknowledged wryly, no Angelos Mena.

She walked down the hallway, checking several spare rooms, before she finally found Sofia in a large, airy room at the end of the hall, its gabled windows overlooking the sea. Sofia was curled up in the wide window seat, looking out at the glittering waters.

'*Kalimera,*' Talia tried as she came into the room. Sofia turned to look at her, smiling shyly although Talia could still see sorrow in her big, dark eyes.

'Hello.'

'We're both learning,' Talia approved. She came to sit on the window seat next to Sofia. 'You have lessons this morning?' With a bit of miming of reading and writing, Talia was able to communicate what she meant, and Sofia nodded.

They sat in silence for a moment before Talia ventured, '*Papa? Yia sou?*' She mimed waving goodbye, and Sofia shook her head.

'Papa…not…say,' she said in halting English.

'He didn't say goodbye?' Talia struggled to keep the dismay from her voice. Sofia shook her head again.

'*Ohi*…no. But…' She pointed to a sheet of paper in her lap, the single page filled with strong, slanting handwriting.

'He wrote you a letter,' Talia surmised, and Sofia nodded.

The letter was in Greek, of course, and Talia would never read someone else's correspondence, yet she found she was intensely curious to know what Angelos had written to his daughter…and why he hadn't said goodbye.

The sound of a motorboat cut through the still air, and Sofia leaned out the window to wave to the woman approaching the dock. 'Ava,' she said, turning back to Talia, and then said something in Greek Talia didn't understand but could guess the nature of.

'Your teacher,' she said, and Sofia repeated the new word.

'Teacher. *Ne.* Yes.'

A few minutes later Ava, a friendly woman in her forties, came upstairs. Fortunately she spoke English, and when Talia had explained who she was she offered to help her learn Greek after her lessons with Sofia.

'I'll have to ask Kyrie Mena,' Talia said, suspecting that Angelos would want to hear about any changes in plan. 'But I'm sure he'd like me to know more Greek.'

Ava laughed knowingly at that and Talia headed downstairs while Sofia had her lessons. Maria had disappeared from the kitchen, and so after standing uncertainly in the spacious hallway for a moment, Talia decided to go outside.

The air was hot and dry even though it was only a little past nine in the morning, and the sun shone brightly above, glinting off the sea.

Talia made her way through the garden, enjoying the colour and scent of the jumble of flowers. The gardens at the estate back in New York were lovely, but in a careful, manicured way. She liked the wildness here, felt its surprising answer in herself.

Funny, really, to think that Angelos Mena, of all people, would have a wild garden. But perhaps he wasn't here enough to keep it in order.

The thought made her frown as she stepped onto the beach, slipping off her sandals so she could feel the warm sand between her toes.

She made her way to the water's edge, letting the warm sea lap at her toes. She imagined Angelos back in Athens, sitting down at some important business meeting, making his so-called swift decisions. Athens was only an hour away, and yet he'd said he wouldn't be back for weeks. Why couldn't he make the trip more often, for Sofia's sake?

Talia knew it wasn't her concern; Angelos had certainly said as much. Besides, she was only here for six weeks, and she could hardly entangle herself in the lives of the Menas.

And yet…thoughts and questions whirled through her mind. The portrait of the secretly smiling woman; the fire Angelos refused to speak about. The sorrow she saw in Sofia's eyes, and the letter that had lain on her lap.

And of course the book. The real reason she was here, she reminded herself, was to find Giovanni's book. Sighing, Talia turned from the beach and headed back up to the villa.

Sofia was still in her lessons so Talia stayed in the kitchen with Maria, watching her as she kneaded bread. She'd offered to help, but Maria had vociferously refused, instead sitting her back down at the table, this time with a cup of what she called mountain tea. Talia took a cautious sip—Maria had made it by boiling what looked like a bunch of stems and leaves in a little brass pot—and found it surprisingly pleasant, a cross between chamomile and peppermint.

'It cures everything,' Maria assured her, 'except heartbreak. But you are not heartbroken, are you?'

'No, definitely not,' Talia assured her.

'You did not come all this way to Greece because of a failed romance?' Maria asked, sounding almost hopeful. Talia smothered a smile at the housekeeper's not so subtle attempt at digging into her past.

'No failed romances,' Talia answered. 'No romances at all, unless you count the boy I dated when I was seventeen.'

'You're waiting for someone special,' Maria said sagely. 'That is good.'

'I think I might be waiting a long time.' Talia shrugged the woman's sympathy aside. 'I've been happy on my own. I still am.'

'Every woman needs a man.'

Talia decided not to argue this point. 'But you don't

want me crawling into Angelos's bed, do you?' she joked, only to flush as Maria eyed her appraisingly.

'It was Kyrie Mena this morning.'

'It still is,' she promised. 'That was a slip. Trust me, I'm not going to be crawling into anyone's bed but my own.' She closed her eyes briefly, wondering if this conversation could actually get any more awkward.

'You do not want to set your sights on Kyrie Mena,' Maria said firmly. She gave the bread dough a few firm kneads. 'He is not a whole man.'

Intrigued, Talia leaned forward. 'Not a whole man?' He certainly looked like a whole man, devastatingly attractive in every part. 'What do you mean by that?'

Maria shook her head. 'I should not have said it. It is only there has been much tragedy in his life. He is not able to give a woman all she would need here.' Maria pressed a hand to her heart.

So Angelos was emotionally repressed? Not exactly a surprise. 'When you say tragedy,' Talia asked, 'do you mean the fire?'

Maria pressed her lips together. 'I should not have said.'

Talia could tell she wasn't going to get anything else out of the housekeeper about that, and so she asked if there was a library instead.

'A library? You want a book?'

'I thought I might see if there was anything to read,' Talia demurred, squashing a feeling of guilt at her duplicity. She did want a book, one specific book. But she had no idea if it was on Kallos, or in Angelos's possession at all.

'There is a room at the top of the house,' Maria said. 'Above the bedrooms. You will find some books there.'

Since Sofia was still busy with her teacher, Talia followed Maria's directions, up a winding staircase to a single, airy room on the top floor, with windows in every direction and bookshelves lining all the walls.

She stood in the centre of the room for a moment, enjoying the view of the sea all around her, before she began to study the books lining the shelves. Angelos had an eclectic collection of books: history, politics, art and music, even a little light fiction. None of the books looked like the one Giovanni had described, handcrafted with a cover of tooled leather.

Sighing, Talia berated herself for hoping it could be so simple. Did she actually think she'd just find the rare book lying on a shelf for anyone to pick up? She didn't know if it was on this island, or even in Angelos's possession. If he did own it, he might well keep it in Athens, in a safe. And maybe he didn't own it. The only way she would know, Talia acknowledged, was by asking the man himself.

She was just about to head back downstairs when Sofia popped her head up over the banister. 'I look for you!' she exclaimed in English, and Talia laughed.

'And you found me. How was your lesson?'

'Good,' Sofia said, and ducked her head in shy pride at how much English she'd spoken. Then she pointed to Talia. 'You now.'

'My Greek lesson?' Talia surmised. 'Bring it on.' She followed Sofia downstairs, where Ava was waiting.

Ten days passed by faster than Talia felt she could blink. It was easy to lose herself in the sunny haze of days; she spent the mornings reading or sketching or simply lazing on the beach, and then had a Greek lesson with Ava. The afternoons were with Sofia, either inside doing crafts or playing games, or outside walking, swimming and exploring some of the island.

She and Sofia managed to communicate through miming and bits of broken English and Greek, improvement showing on both sides with every passing day.

And with each day Talia saw Sofia becoming more confident and comfortable, although whenever Angelos came into the conversation a cloud passed over her face, and shadows came into her eyes. Talia started trying to keep her employer out of the conversation, even as her heart ached for Sofia and the lack of a loving parent in her life.

Several times she tried to find out more information about her grandfather's book, but when she asked Maria if Angelos liked poetry, she received an utterly blank look.

'Poetry? No.'

'He seems an educated man,' Talia tried. 'He has so many books upstairs… I thought he might enjoy a bit of poetry.'

'Are we talking about the same Kyrie Mena?' Maria asked with raised eyebrows. 'The man I know does not like poetry. He certainly doesn't read it.' Her gaze narrowed as she glanced at Talia. 'Why do you ask?'

'No reason,' Talia answered with a weak smile, guilt flashing through her. In the ten days since she'd arrived on Kallos she'd grown close to both Maria and Sofia, and Ava as well. She hated the thought that she was deceiving anyone, but she didn't know how to admit the truth without hurting everyone involved, and potentially enraging her boss.

Although she tried not to talk to Sofia about Angelos, Talia spent an inordinate amount of time wondering about him. How long had he been a widower? Had he loved his wife very much? Sometimes she would pause in the dining room and gaze up at the portrait of Xanthe Mena, with her heavy-lidded look and small, secretive smile, and wonder what she'd been like, and how she'd captured the heart of her husband.

Not that she was concerned about Angelos Mena's heart, Talia told herself. She was just curious. It was only natural.

Ten days into her time on Kallos her grandfather wrote her an email, asking about the book. Talia read the few lines with a growing sense of guilt, because she knew that she'd only made a few half-hearted attempts to find out any information.

When Angelos returned, she decided, she'd ask him about the book flat out. She'd try, at least.

Quickly she typed an email back to Giovanni.

Dear Nonno,
I am doing my best. I hope to have news soon. But please don't worry about me. I am having a good time and I hope you are keeping well.
Love, Talia.

For a second she pictured him in the conservatory where they'd shared so many meals, and a wave of homesickness washed over her. He'd become so frail in the last few months, his once robust and commanding figure diminished by age and illness. She hated the thought that she was missing time with him, precious days and weeks she'd never have again.

Which made her more determined than ever to find his book.

She was just pressing Send when she heard a distant whirring. She left her laptop open on her bed and hurried to the window, where she saw a helicopter touch down on the helipad. Her heart seemed to leap in her throat as the hatch opened and a familiar figure stepped out before striding down the path to the house.

Angelos Mena was home.

# CHAPTER SIX

HE HADN'T MEANT to come back. Angelos Mena headed down the garden path, half inclined to turn around and climb back into the helicopter. He hadn't been intending to return to Kallos for another two weeks at least.

But he'd found himself thinking about returning almost since the moment he'd left. He wanted to make sure Talia Di Sione was indeed a suitable nanny, and even though Maria had assured him in several emails that she was, Angelos needed to see for himself. His daughter's welfare was paramount.

At least that was why he told himself he was back so soon. He just didn't completely believe it.

Now he stepped into the quiet of the villa, breathed in the scents of bougainvillea and heliotrope from outside. Maria hurried towards him.

'Kyrie Mena! I was not expecting you. You didn't send word you were coming.'

'It was a last-minute decision,' Angelos said as he shed his suit jacket. 'I'm sorry if I've inconvenienced you.'

'Not at all,' Maria clucked, bustling around him as she always did. 'I will make up your bedroom. And as for dinner…?'

Angelos hesitated. He normally didn't stay on Kallos for many meals, and those he took were by his desk, working. 'Have you eaten?' he asked. Maria shook her head.

'No, not yet. We were just going to have something simple in the kitchen…'

'Then I will join you for dinner.' Maria looked flummoxed; Angelos never joined them in the kitchen.

'Very good, sir,' she murmured, and he turned away, towards the solitude of his study.

He worked until he heard Sofia and Talia come downstairs; he listened to their chatter, a pidgin mixture of English and Greek, punctuated by much laughter. He couldn't remember the last time he'd heard his daughter sound so excited, so happy.

The realisation felt like a fist clenching his heart.

Finally when he could hear Maria putting the meal on the table he rose from his desk and went into the kitchen. The moment he stepped into the doorway the room fell silent, and three heads swivelled expectantly towards him.

*'Kalispera,'* Angelos greeted them, his voice terser than he would have liked. 'You are all well?'

'Very well,' Maria answered when no one else seemed inclined to say anything. Angelos sat down at the table and after a brief pause Talia and Sofia joined him there.

'Hello, Papa,' Sofia whispered, and Angelos smiled at her. She ducked her head, letting her hair fall forward to hide her scarred cheek. Everything inside him tightened in regret and dismay, and he looked away to compose himself. His interactions with Sofia were always like this.

As he put his napkin in his lap he could feel Talia watching him, and when he looked up he saw how she was gazing at him in what almost seemed like disapproval, her lips pursed, her eyes narrowed.

He raised his eyebrows in silent enquiry, and flushing, she looked away.

She looked good, he noticed. The last week had left her

tanned, the freckles across her nose coming out in bold relief. Her hair had golden streaks, and she seemed more relaxed than she had a week ago, even if she seemed determined to give him a death stare all dinner long.

The meal was awful. The food was as delicious as always, but the conversation was stilted and awkward, punctuated by long, taut silences. Whenever Angelos asked Sofia a question she stammered or mumbled an answer, and then hung her head.

Talia didn't speak at all, but Angelos could feel the censure and even the animosity rolling off her in waves and when the plates were cleared Angelos decided he had had enough of it. He excused himself before dessert was served, claiming he needed to work.

Back in his study he paced the room before he reached for the bottle of ouzo he kept in a drinks cabinet and poured himself a small measure. Then he cursed and slammed the glass back onto the desk. Alcohol was not the answer.

He went to his laptop, but he'd finished writing his notes on the last consultancy and he'd done nearly all the prep work on his next client. He had an unprecedented five days to spend at his leisure, and the truth was he didn't know what to do with it. At least when he worked he didn't have time to think. To remember.

He was staring blindly into the empty hearth when a quiet knock sounded at the door.

Angelos stiffened. No one disturbed him in his study. Maria knew it was off-limits, and Sofia would never dare. Which left one person who could be knocking at his door, one person who dared to disturb his privacy.

'Enter,' he barked, and the door swung open to reveal Talia standing there, her hands on her hips, her eyes blazing.

\* \* \*

Talia was furious. She'd been furious ever since Angelos's helicopter had landed three hours ago, and he hadn't even come upstairs to say hello to his daughter.

When he'd appeared for dinner, she'd managed to calm down a little. Maybe he really was busy with work. He'd come back earlier than he'd intended, and he was making the effort to have a meal with them. She was willing to be appeased, even impressed. But then his behaviour during that meal—the bitten-off questions, the stony looks—had made her fury return in full force. And no matter what happened, even if the man fired her, she knew she couldn't stay silent any longer. For Sofia's sake she had to speak.

'Did you need something?' Angelos asked, his tone as curt as ever. He looked devastatingly sexy standing there, with the top two buttons of his crisp white shirt unbuttoned, revealing the tanned column of his throat, and the sleeves rolled up to show his powerful forearms. His hair was slightly mussed, and a five-o'clock shadow glinted on his strong jaw. Just the sight of him was enough to make every thought empty out of Talia's head, and she had a hard time remembering why she was so angry.

'I thought,' Angelos continued as he turned to his desk, effectively dismissing her, 'that Maria would have told you my study is off-limits.'

'You mean you're off-limits,' Talia returned. She was fast recalling her fury, especially when Angelos didn't even look up as he answered her. No matter how sexy the man was, he could still act like an ass.

'When I am working, yes.'

She gestured to his closed laptop. 'Have you been working, Kyrie Mena?'

Angelos glanced up then, clearly annoyed by her challenge. 'What is it you want, Miss Di Sione?'

'I thought you were going to call me Talia,' she reminded him with acid sweetness. 'Not that you've ever asked me to call you by your first name.'

'I am your employer.'

Talia rolled her eyes. 'You are also the most stiff and formal man I've ever met. In this day and age, I think it would be perfectly appropriate for us to call each other by our first names.'

He looked utterly nonplussed by this apparently outrageous suggestion. 'Is this why you came into my study? To discuss how we address each other?'

'No.' Talia let out her breath in a huff. She was picking the wrong fight, but there was so much about Angelos and his distant, disdainful attitude that got up her nose. Made her want to come out swinging for Sofia's sake. 'But I thought I'd mention it, as an aside.'

'Fine. You've mentioned it.' He turned away again and Talia clenched her hands into fists.

'You know, I *think* you love your daughter,' she said, her voice shaking with the force of her feeling, 'but I wouldn't be able to tell from your behaviour. At all.'

Angelos turned around slowly. His face was blank, his eyes like two dark pools, his huge body radiating menace. Talia felt a tremor of trepidation go through her; she'd already learned that Angelos was at his most terrifying when she couldn't tell anything from his expression.

'I have no interest in what you think,' he said, enunciating each harsh word with cold precision. 'And no desire for you to come and invade my privacy with your ridiculous presumption.'

She blinked, half amazed at the blatant insults he delivered with such deliberate cruelty, even as part of her recognised it as a tactic. A defence, and one she was determined to break through. 'You really are incredibly rude,' she told him, glad her voice came out evenly. 'As well as—dare I say it?—*short-sighted*. I spend more time with your daughter than anyone else does. Maybe you should care what I think.'

Two spots of colour appeared high on Angelos's sharp cheekbones, but his expression remained glacial, his eyes like chips of dark ice. 'You overstep yourself, Miss Di Sione,' he said, his voice a quiet, warning hiss. Talia felt a tremble of fear, and yet courage or perhaps just a deep conviction of what Sofia needed propelled her onwards.

'So what are you going to do, fire me?' she demanded as she took a step towards him, felt the heat from his body and inhaled the clean male scent of him. 'I'm overstepping myself because I care about your daughter. And your behaviour hurts her terribly, even though she tries to hide it. Why can't you be more—' She broke off, searching for a word, and Angelos raised his eyebrows, his whole body tensed with suppressed fury.

'Be more what?' he asked, biting off each word and spitting it out.

'*Loving*,' she burst out. 'She's a little girl. She has so few people in her life. She wants to be loved by her papa.'

Her words seemed to echo in the taut stillness of the room, and for one brief second Angelos's features twisted in what looked like a grimace of anguish, and Talia felt as if her heart was suspended in her chest as realisation slammed into her. *He was hurting...just as Sofia was hurting.*

Just as she was hurting.

Then his expression ironed out and he turned away, busying himself with some papers on his desk, his back to her.

'This conversation is over.'

'Angelos...' It was the first time she'd dared to call him

by his first name, and it felt weirdly intimate, as if she had just used an endearment. She took a step towards him, reaching a hand out, wanting to touch him, to offer him that little comfort, and her too. She imagined the feel of his shoulder under her palm, hot and hard and strong. She craved that connection, however brief and illusory it was, and she imagined, foolishly perhaps, he craved it too. Yet even so she didn't dare. 'Surely someone else,' she said quietly, 'Maria or one of the nannies, has spoken to you about this? Has been as concerned as I have?'

'The other nannies were not nearly as interested in Sofia as you seem to be,' Angelos answered tonelessly. 'Now I wonder if that was no bad thing.' He glanced up at her, his expression as cold and implacable as it ever had been, and Talia knew any moment of connection she had been hoping for was well and truly severed. 'I am not asking for your opinion on these matters. You are here for a short time only, Talia. You are not part of our lives. In a month you will be gone from here, as good as forgotten.'

The deliberate brutality of his words felt like a slap to the face, a fist to the gut. She blinked rapidly, startled by how hurt she felt by Angelos's cold statement. She may have only been on Kallos for ten days, but she felt as if she'd become part of Sofia's life, as if she *mattered*. And, Talia realised with a stab of remorse, she mattered to so few people in her life. Her grandfather, her brothers and sisters…her circle of loved ones was incredibly small. She hadn't thought she minded, but now…

'That may be true,' she managed when she trusted her voice not to tremble with the force of her hurt. 'But I'm part of Sofia's life now. I matter to her *now*, and she matters to me.' Angelos simply stared, blatantly unimpressed. Talia fought the urge to cry, or maybe scream. She felt as if she were banging her head against a wall. A very hard wall. Maybe Angelos was right, and she should just stop. It wasn't as if she'd ever see these people again after the next month. Why was she pushing so much? Why did she care so much?

*Because you know how Sofia feels.*

She took a deep breath and forced all the feelings back. 'How long are you staying for this time?' she asked, and she saw surprise flicker across Angelos's face at the abrupt change in topic.

'I have not yet decided. I came to make sure you were doing an adequate job—'

'And am I?'

'That remains to be seen,' Angelos answered coolly. 'Now, as I said before, this conversation is—'

'Perhaps you should assess my performance,' Talia suggested before she lost her courage. She felt reckless now, almost wild; he'd already hurt her so what did she really have to lose? 'Surely you need to see if I really am doing the thing properly. *Appropriately.*' Angelos narrowed his eyes, clearly trying to figure out her game. Talia gave him her sunniest smile, even though she felt fragile inside, ready to break. 'Tomorrow Sofia and I are going on a picnic,' she stated, although she hadn't planned any such thing. 'I've been wanting to walk to the far side of the island. Why don't you come with us?'

He stared at her for a long moment, a muscle flickering in his jaw, his eyes utterly opaque. Talia waited for his answer, her breath held, trying not to hope too hard.

'Well played, Miss Di Sione,' he finally said, and there was a faint note of reluctant admiration in his voice that made Talia release her breath in a relieved rush. 'You are a positive terrier.'

'I'll take that as a compliment.'

'It wasn't necessarily meant as one.' Angelos turned

back to his desk, bracing his hands flat on the burnished surface, almost as if he were steeling himself—but for what? 'As tempting as a picnic sounds,' he said, 'I'm afraid I will have to forego such pleasures. I have a lot of work to do.'

'Why did you come back at all, then?' Talia demanded, hurt audible in her voice, making her cringe. She'd thought he'd been going to accept, and the intense disappointment she felt at his refusal felt like an overreaction, yet one she couldn't keep herself from.

'I told you—'

'To assess my capabilities? But you haven't spent any time with me or Sofia. How can you possibly know how capable I am?'

He swung around, anger igniting in his eyes again, making them burn. 'Why are you so damnably persistent?'

'Because I know what it's like to be without a father,' Talia confessed. She felt the blood rush to her face at this unwarranted admission. 'Or a mother. I lost both my parents when I was a year old.'

Angelos stared at her for a long moment, his jaw bunched, his arms still folded, and yet Talia sensed a softening in him. 'I'm sorry,' he finally said, his voice gruff. 'I would not wish that on anyone.'

'Sofia's already lost her mother,' Talia pressed while she had an advantage. 'She needs you—'

'And she has me.' He cut her off swiftly, his tone and expression hardening once more. 'I provide for her every need, and I visit here as often as I can. And frankly, Miss Di Sione, Sofia is better off without me around.' He swung away again, driving a hand through his hair, his back, taut and quivering with tension, to her. 'Now, go please,' he said in a low voice. 'Before either of us says something we will later regret.'

Talia stared at him for a long moment, everything in her wanting to go comfort this man. She sensed a grief and even a darkness in him that she hadn't expected, and it called to a similar emotion in her that she'd long suppressed.

'Angelos...' she tried, hesitantly, because they did not remotely have the kind of relationship that would allow her to offer comfort, and she wasn't sure she wanted to give it anyway. Reaching out to this man, actually connecting with him, would be dangerous for both of them.

And yet she stayed, even lifted her hand as she had before, fingers trembling, straining... Her fingertips brushed his shoulder, and she felt his muscles quiver and jerk in response, or perhaps she was the one who moved, a jolt running through her body that surprised her with its impossible force. She'd barely touched him.

'Go,' Angelos said, his voice low and insistent, his head bowed, and dropping her hand, her whole body reacting to that tiny touch, Talia went.

Angelos stayed in his study working until the small hours of the morning. Better to work and try to blot out all the damning accusations Talia had hurled at him. The pleas to spend time with his daughter, when that was the one thing he couldn't do.

For a second, staring blankly at the page of notes he'd been making on his new client, Angelos remembered what it had been like to be close to Sofia. To hold the warm baby weight of her in his arms, tuck her head against his shoulder and rest his chin on top of her silky hair. He remembered how she'd always tugged on his ears, giving a great big baby's belly laugh. How Xanthe had watched them, smiling that secret smile, love shining in her eyes...

With a curse he shoved the pad of paper away, driving

his hands through his hair, his nails raking his scalp, as if he could push the memories right out of his head. As if he could change the past, the night that had claimed Xanthe's life and scarred Sofia for ever. The night that had been his fault.

He glanced at the ouzo in the drinks cabinet, and then turned away.

The house was quiet as he headed upstairs, the night breeze cool. He paused outside Talia's room, wondering how she'd taken his rebuttals. He'd been harsh, he knew, but she'd been so damnably determined. She'd been trying to make him see, and the trouble was, he saw all too clearly. He saw that when he was near his daughter he made her uncomfortable, reminded her of all they'd lost. Sofia might need a father, but she needed a better one than him.

And yet Talia didn't know that, didn't realise how unworthy he was. She'd tried to comfort him, and for a second, his eyes clenched shut, Angelos remembered the feel of her fingers on his shoulder, barely the brush of a hand, and yet it had made him feel as if his skin had been scraped raw, every nerve exposed to stinging air. Not a pleasant feeling, and yet it had made him feel so *alive*. For a second he'd craved even more; the kind of connection to another human being that he hadn't had in seven years. It would have felt like the ripping of a bandage from a wound, the sudden exposure to light and air and life, painful and necessary and good.

And not for him.

Banishing all thoughts of Talia, he moved past her room to Sofia's, slipping inside silently as he did every night he was on Kallos, while his daughter slept.

Sofia lay on her side, her knees tucked up as they always were. As Angelos came closer, his throat constricted as he saw the dried traces of tears on his daughter's cheek.

She'd been crying…because of him? Because of what he had or hadn't done? He glanced down and saw the last letter he'd written her on the floor, having slipped from her fingers as she'd fallen asleep.

Guilt lashed him, a scourge whose sting he accepted as his due. Sofia's sadness was his fault. He knew that. He'd always known that. He just didn't know how he could make it better.

'*S'agapo manaria mou,*' he said softly, and then, as he always did, he slipped silently from the room before she could wake.

Talia woke the next morning determined to give Sofia the day she should have had with her father, if he'd only been willing. She asked Maria to pack a picnic, and, a few games to play on the beach and plenty of sun cream.

As soon as Sofia had finished her lessons, she announced her intentions.

'A picnic?' Sofia's face lit up as she smiled shyly. Talia had noticed how quiet and downhearted she'd seemed since Angelos's arrival yesterday afternoon, and she was glad to see the girl brightening now. 'Just…just the two of us?' She glanced inadvertently towards her father's study, the door firmly closed.

'Yes,' Talia said, injecting as much cheer as she could into her voice. 'Won't it be fun? I've been wanting to explore the other side of the island. We can swim on the other beach.' Sofia frowned in confusion, and with exaggerated movements Talia mimed what she meant. She deserved an Academy Award for her acting talents, she thought wryly as Sofia nodded in understanding.

Talia slathered them both in sun cream, and cramming the wide straw hat she'd borrowed from Maria on her head, she headed outside with Sofia.

The sky was cloudless blue, the sun already high and hot above, and the other side of the island beckoned enticingly. Kallos wasn't very big, a few square miles at most, but Talia hadn't ventured much beyond the landscaped gardens and beach right in front of the villa.

Now, despite the disappointment caused by Angelos's absence, she found she was looking forward to seeing a little more of the island. The sense of adventure that had been dormant for so long rose up once more, so she walked with a spring in her step as they left the bright tangle of the villa's gardens for the stony hill above the house.

They'd just crested the hill and Talia was gazing in interest at the rock-strewn valley below when Sofia suddenly exclaimed in Greek.

Afraid she'd seen a snake or something dangerous, Talia whirled around. Sofia was pointing back towards the villa.

'Papa,' she exclaimed.

Talia held up her hand to shade her eyes from the sun, and her heart felt as if it had leapt into her throat when she saw Angelos coming up the hill they'd just climbed with long, purposeful strides.

'Papa,' she agreed cautiously, and she glanced down at Sofia to see a look of apprehension coming over her face as Angelos drew nearer. He was dressed as casually as she'd ever seen him, in shorts that emphasised his powerful thighs and calves and a T-shirt that clung to the well-defined muscles of his chest. He was also, Talia saw as her heart sunk from her throat to her toes, scowling ferociously.

# CHAPTER SEVEN

TALIA AND SOFIA watched Angelos climb up the hill, his stride easy and powerful, the scowl on his face deepening with every step. Sofia slid her hand into Talia's and hid slightly behind her.

Talia lifted her chin, determined to brazen out whatever Angelos had in mind. What on earth could he be angry about? Taking his daughter on a picnic?

'Well.' He stood in front of them, his hands on his hips, the scowl still on his face. 'I'm here.'

'So you are,' Talia agreed warily. 'Why?'

His gaze snapped to hers, his eyes widening in disbelief. 'Did you not ask me to come on a picnic, even though it is a wretchedly hot day? And so I came.'

Talia simply stared at him for a long moment before she finally realised what he was saying. 'You mean…you're coming with us? And you're…you're not angry?'

'Angry?' Angelos stared at her, nonplussed. 'Why do you think I am angry?'

A grin split her face as relief zinged through her. 'Maybe you should look in a mirror on occasion,' she dared to tease. 'You've been scowling the whole time you were climbing the hill, and scaring the dickens out of your daughter and me.'

For a second Angelos looked almost embarrassed.

'Well.' He rubbed his chin, looking away. 'Like I said, it is very hot out here.'

And then the full realisation of what he'd done bloomed inside her, and she felt caught between laughter and tears. Angelos was coming on their picnic. He was *trying*, and maybe that was what had brought the scowl to his face, because this was unfamiliar territory, and it was hard. Harder, perhaps, than Talia even knew.

He was coming out of his comfort zone, and she admired him for it. She knew how incredibly hard that could be.

'We're glad you're here,' she said, and stepped aside so Sofia couldn't hide behind her any longer. 'Aren't we, Sofia?'

*'Ne,'* Sofia answered after a moment, ducking her head so her hair hid her face. Talia suppressed the urge to tuck it behind Sofia's ears; she knew it was a defence mechanism, and one she employed whenever she was in her father's presence.

'Good.' Angelos's expression clouded as he saw the way Sofia hid, but then he gave one brisk nod and surveyed the valley before them. 'So where are you intending to have this picnic?'

'I thought we could walk to the far side of the island. There are some rocks there that look interesting.' Talia pointed to some large boulders that bordered the shoreline, perfect for scrambling.

'Very well.' Angelos nodded again, and Talia had to smother a laugh as she realised how out of his element he was. He had the most commanding, confident presence of anyone she'd encountered, and yet he was clearly out of his depth here, no doubt trying to manage a picnic like a business meeting. 'Shall we?'

'Yes, we shall,' she agreed, and she must not have been

able to keep a teasing note from her voice because Angelos gave her a swift, suspicious look before he started down towards the valley.

They walked down the hill towards the opposite shore; the hillside was dotted with the ancient, gnarled trunks of olive trees, the ground strewn with stones. Talia stumbled on one, and before she'd even had a chance to right herself, Angelos steadied her with one strong hand on her elbow, the touch of his skin against hers a shock to her system just as it had been last night, like being doused in ice water, or jolted with electricity.

Except, Talia reflected as Angelos dropped his hand and they walked on, both of those sensations were unpleasant and Angelos's touch hadn't been unpleasant at all. Far from it. The few times his skin had brushed hers she'd felt a warmth blooming inside her, spreading outward, taking over. It was the kind of feeling that made her want more, made her wonder how to get it.

She was still feeling the aftershocks of his hand on her elbow as they approached the shore, little zinging sensations arrowing low down in her belly. Amazing how a hand on her elbow of all places could make her feel so... tingly. Dangerous too, because she knew she couldn't entertain some kind of crush or attraction for her boss. For a whole lot of reasons.

Not least of all the complication of Giovanni's book. But she didn't want to think about the book today, or how she was going to bring up the subject with Angelos. She just wanted to enjoy their time together, as Sofia was.

She looked down at Sofia walking between them, her shy glance darting from Talia to Angelos, as if she couldn't believe they were both here. And in truth, Talia couldn't believe it. She'd spent hours last night, lying on her bed, staring into the darkness and wondering what Angelos had meant, saying Sofia was better off without him around.

How could he, how could any father, think such a thing? Talia knew what it was like to grow up motherless, fatherless, longing for so much as a memory of the parents she'd had and having only an empty space in her heart and head instead.

She knew her parents hadn't been perfect, far from it. Her oldest brother, Alessandro, had hard memories of her mother and father, memories he wouldn't speak of to anyone, or at least not to Talia. She knew her father had had an affair, which had resulted in a half-brother she barely knew, Nate.

But surely any parents were better than none? Sometimes she and her sister Bianca, who had only a few shadowy memories of their mother—the smell of perfume, the jingle of bracelets—talked about how they missed their parents, missed having ever known them. Missed having a memory of a conversation or cuddle. Giovanni was wonderful, but he'd been only one old and sometimes ill man to care for seven very different and sometimes difficult children.

So why did Angelos shy away from his daughter? Last night, when she'd been in his study and heard the anguish in his voice, seen it in his face for a moment, Talia had been sure there was some private torment that kept Angelos from his daughter, and she'd longed to know what it was, so she could try to relieve him of such an awful burden.

But who was she, she'd asked herself in the darkness of her bedroom last night, to relieve anyone of anything? She'd chosen a life of isolation rather than brave the world around her. She wasn't in any position to offer advice.

*But you're different. You're protecting yourself physi-*

*cally. Angelos is cutting himself off from the person he loves.*

'Shall we stop here?' Angelos asked, and Talia blinked the world into focus. She'd been so lost in her thoughts she'd barely been aware of the island around her, the sea shimmering with sunlight, the boulders they'd reached pointing proudly to a hard, blue sky.

'Yes, this looks good.' Talia took the blanket from her bag and spread it over a patch of even sand. Sofia sat down, kicking off her sandals and then digging her toes into the sand with a sigh of pleasure.

Angelos sat nearby, his long, muscular legs stretched out in front him, his arms braced behind him, as he gazed out at the sea.

'Now this isn't so bad, is it?' Talia teased, and he shot her a dark look.

'It's hot. But the breeze is pleasant.'

'You know I'm not talking about the weather.'

'No.' His forehead furrowed, he glanced at Sofia, who was now kneeling in the sand, scooping it up in handfuls.

'How about we make a sandcastle?' Talia suggested, waving a bucket, and clearly taking her meaning, Sofia clapped her hands. Angelos looked nonplussed.

'A what?'

'A sandcastle? You have made one, haven't you, when you were a child at least?'

'No, not as a child.' He drew his legs up and rested his forearms on his knees, his expression becoming distant and veiled. 'I… I used to make them with Sofia.' He glanced at his daughter, who was watching him warily, not understanding the English. 'But she'd always eat the sand.'

'I'm assuming she was a baby at the time?' Talia said. She was oddly moved by the arrested look on Angelos's face, the sense that this was a precious memory, and one he didn't access often. Again she felt that sense of grief and even torment, so private it felt as if she were glimpsing something she wasn't meant to see, an emotional peeping Tom.

'Yes, she was a baby,' Angelos said, and he looked away. 'Not quite a year old.'

No one spoke, and Talia tried to think of something to say, some way to bridge the moment between darkness and light, between painful memory and carefree present.

Then Angelos turned back to them and gave his daughter a rusty smile, his gaze deliberately averted from Talia. 'Do we have a spade?'

Talia handed him a plastic shovel, her heart precariously full as she watched Angelos begin to dig. They were merely making a sandcastle, and yet it felt like they were building something more, the beginning of something important, its foundation the memories that had gone before.

After a few minutes of them all working together Talia scooted back, content to let father and daughter create their palace. She started to unpack the food Maria had made them, casting a glance every so often to Angelos and Sofia. Neither of them was speaking, so she couldn't say it was a huge bonding success, but at least they were doing something together. It still felt like a lot.

Carefully Angelos turned the bucket over and lifted it so a perfect dome of damp sand emerged. Sofia peeped up at him, a shy smile lighting her features, making the old guilt and grief inside him twist painfully. He could tell his daughter was pleased to have him here, and it made him wonder if he'd been remiss, even wrong, in staying away for so long.

But he'd felt he'd had no choice. He'd honestly believed he was doing the best thing for Sofia. And maybe he had been. A single, sunny afternoon was simply that. A moment in time. The reality of his presence in Sofia's life was that he was inept, inexperienced, and it brought back painful reminders of everything his daughter didn't have.

He glanced at Talia, who had unpacked several containers of food and was now sitting on the edge of the blanket, her hands clasped around her knees as she stared out at the sea. Her hair blew in tangles around her face, making Angelos itch to tuck it behind her ears, let his fingers skim the silky softness of her cheek.

His insides clenched at the thought as he grimly acknowledged that he was attracted to his temporary nanny. Ironic, really, that he'd had his choice of svelte beauties before and he'd always refused them. He hadn't felt so much as a flicker of desire for the other nannies, not to mention the women at work and in Athens who had offered themselves to him. It had been so long he'd wondered if his libido had simply gone for good. He hadn't even minded; life was simpler that way, and pleasure was something he hadn't so much as considered in a long, long time.

But since Talia Di Sione had catapulted into his life, his libido had become positively wakeful. Desire had roared through him last night when she'd touched his shoulder. His *shoulder*. For heaven's sake, it wasn't as if she'd rubbed up against him, or tried to kiss him, those petal-soft lips opening and yielding under his...

At these thoughts his body stirred to life and Angelos shifted where he sat. What was he doing, thinking like this?

Talia caught his glance and smiled at him. Sofia was busy completing her castle, and so they had a moment of private conversation.

'So you didn't make sandcastles as a child? How come?'

Jolted by the question, as well as the nature of his own

recent thoughts, Angelos answered without thinking. 'I had no opportunity. I grew up in Piraeus.'

'Piraeus?' Talia wrinkled her nose. 'But isn't that near the beach?'

Angelos shook his head, wishing he hadn't said so much. He never talked about his childhood, not even to Xanthe. She hadn't wanted to know, had preferred to think they were starting something new and better together. 'The docks,' he explained succinctly. And then, for no reason he could fathom except that Talia was looking at him with such honest, interested curiosity, he clarified, 'I was a street rat.'

'A street rat?' Her eyebrows rose in disbelief even as her expression clouded with sympathy. 'What do you mean exactly?'

Angelos shrugged. 'I was—am—an orphan. My father was never around and my mother gave me up when I was a baby. I grew up in a home for children, but when I was fourteen I left to work on the docks.' He looked away, not wanting to see the revulsion and pity he knew would be in her eyes. Xanthe had been horrified by his past. She'd accepted it, accepted him, but she'd wanted to pretend the ugly parts of his story didn't exist. And so Angelos had acted as if they hadn't.

'That's terrible,' Talia said quietly. 'And it must have been so hard for you. I'm so, so sorry.'

Her obvious sincerity left him feeling nonplussed, even disoriented. 'I survived.'

'But how did you go from working the docks to owning your own management consultancy?' she asked. She sounded quietly awed, which made no sense. Angelos turned back, still expecting to see pity, and instead he saw admiration shining in her eyes.

It felt like a kick to the gut, to the heart. Suddenly he

was breathless. 'I had a lot of luck,' he said gruffly. 'I went to night school and received my high school accreditation, and then a scholarship to university. I started my own firm fifteen years ago, a single room in a shabby building in the wrong part of Athens.'

'That doesn't sound like luck,' Talia said. 'That sounds like a lot of hard work and determination.'

Angelos just shrugged again. He didn't know how to handle her admiration; he was so unused to it. Xanthe had met him when he was already successful, and the people from his past had disappeared a long time ago. In any case, he didn't deserve it, not really. So he'd worked hard. He'd made money. What did it matter? He hadn't been able to protect his family at the most crucial time. He hadn't been able to save his wife.

'Angelos, I'm proud of you,' Talia said, laying a hand on his arm. He tensed beneath her touch, every nerve twanging to life from the simple brush of her fingers. He had a mad, nearly irresistible urge to pull her into his arms and plunder the soft mouth he hadn't been able to stop looking at. No one had ever said they were proud of him, not even Xanthe.

Talia's fingers tightened on his arm and Angelos felt his insides coil in expectation. It would be so easy to turn to her, to take her face in his hands and draw her lovely mouth towards his. Everything in him pulsed with the desire to do so.

And he sensed that she wanted him to, that she wouldn't resist. The attraction was mutual, which both excited and alarmed him. It would be so, so easy...

Then Sofia turned from her finished sandcastle, chattering to Talia, and she let her hand slip from his arm. Angelos let out a long, low, silent breath of relief—and disappointment. The moment, whatever it had been, had passed.

Talia started putting food on plastic plates, and handing them around, and after a few seconds when his libido lay down again, Angelos rejoined the conversation.

He picked at the delicious offerings of cheese and bread and olives, a restlessness inside him that he'd quieted for a long time, and this not to do with the overwhelming physical attraction he had for his nanny. This was caused by something deeper, something more emotional. At first he hadn't liked Talia's prying questions, but then part of him had. Part of him had been glad to share something of who he was, to be honest and open with another person.

Disturbed by this thought, he put the plate aside and started walking towards the sea. He kicked off his sandals and let the cool water lap over his feet, cool his blood. What was *wrong* with him today?

From behind him he could hear Talia clearing the dishes, talking to Sofia. Then he heard them both coming across the sand, and he saw that Sofia had stripped to her one-piece and Talia…

Every thought flew out of his head as he gazed at Talia in a forest-green bikini. It was, for a bikini, quite modest: boy shorts and a halter top. He was able to acknowledge that even as his pulse skyrocketed and his mouth dried, his gaze moving inexorably towards the gentle swell of her breasts under the thin fabric, the enticing dip of her waist and flare of her hips. His palms ached to smooth across her golden skin, to anchor her hips in his hands….

Horrified by how quickly he'd envisioned that fantasy, how instantly his blood had heated and his body had responded, Angelos stripped off his shirt and dived cleanly into the sea, letting the shock of the cold water cool his response.

'How is it, Papa?' Sofia asked, and Angelos stood, making sure he was waist-deep to hide any lingering effects of seeing Talia.

'Cold but fine,' he called. 'Why don't you come in?'

He told himself not to so much as glance at Talia, but clearly his body was not receiving his brain's signals because his gaze slid that way, and he inhaled sharply as he saw the desire in her eyes. Watched her gaze drop to his bare chest before flicking away.

So he'd been right. She wanted him. She wanted him just as he wanted her.

The realisation shocked him, not because he was so surprised that Talia would desire him physically, but because it had been so long since he'd felt the same. And for a second, no more, he considered acting on the attraction they both felt.

It could be simple, if they let it be. She was here only for six weeks; they could have a fling, get each other out of their systems. The sex would be good, fantastic even, and it had been so *long…*

And what about Sofia? In the last twenty-four hours he'd seen how Sofia was happier, more confident and comfortable, with Talia around. He could not risk his daughter's well-being simply to scratch an itch he'd only just developed.

He turned away from Talia, effectively ignoring her as she dove into the water, and watched Sofia instead.

Angelos Mena in nothing but shorts was an unbearably gorgeous sight. Talia knew she was probably making a fool of herself, letting her gaze linger on his broad, bronzed chest, watching the muscles in his shoulders and arms ripple enticingly as he held his hands out to Sofia. His stomach was perfectly flat, every contour of his six-pack abs defined.

She imagined brushing her fingers against those ridged muscles, exploring their shape, letting her hand slide lower...

A blush scorched her cheeks as she realised what she was imagining. She, who had absolutely no bedroom experience, hadn't done anything but buss lips with a boy a lifetime ago, was picturing *that*? She didn't even know what *that* would look like. Feel like.

Quickly Talia ducked her head under the water, kicking hard away from Angelos and Sofia. She had to shut down this line of thinking now. She couldn't bear the thought of Angelos seeing the overwhelming desire she felt in her face. What if he sent her away, suspecting she was trying to seduce him?

The thought that she could seduce anyone, much less a man as powerful and commanding as Angelos, was utterly absurd. He would never be attracted to someone like her, someone with absolutely zero worldly experience.

She thought of that portrait in the dining room, the elegant sophistication of the woman who had been his wife, with her dark eyes and knowing smile. Whereas she didn't know anything.

Suddenly, to her shock, she felt strong hands close around her shoulders like iron bands and she was jerked out of the sea, coughing and sputtering as she inhaled a mouthful of salt water.

'Why did you swim underwater for so long?' Angelos demanded. His face was thrust close to hers, his eyes glittering with fury, droplets of water beading on his bare chest.

'I don't know... I was just swimming.' Her body pressed

close to his, Talia could barely form a coherent thought. She could feel his thighs against hers, hard and powerful, his hands still clasping her shoulders, her breasts brushing his chest, making them tighten and ache.

'I thought you'd hit your head or something when you dove in,' Angelos gritted out. 'I couldn't see you...'

Despite the desire swirling through her like a delicious fog, Talia could tell Angelos had been genuinely worried.

'I'm sorry,' she said. 'I've always liked swimming. I grew up by the water. You don't need to worry about me in the water.'

He released her so suddenly she nearly fell backwards. She found her footing as Angelos stepped back, his expression shuttering. 'Next time come up for air a little sooner,' he bit out, and then turned away, back to Sofia, who was paddling in the shallows.

Talia watched them together, wondering at Angelos's extreme reaction. All right, she may have been underwater for a little while, but she'd always liked swimming, the way the water cocooned her, made her feel safe. And she'd been trying to get over her physical reaction to her boss.

Unfortunately Angelos's manhandling of her had only made it worse. Her arms burned where he'd touched her, and every part of her tingled. The peaks of her breasts ached where they'd brushed against his bare chest.

Best not to think of that again, Talia told herself, and dove back under the water, making sure to resurface before Angelos came looking for her again.

They stayed on the beach for most of the afternoon, swimming and lazing around, but Angelos didn't attempt to make conversation again beyond a few basic pleasantries.

Talia knew it was better that way, and yet the little

he'd said about his childhood had provided an intriguing glimpse into the emotional interior of a man who had, on appearance, always seemed hard and cold and, frankly, unfriendly.

It made her want to get to know him more, but Angelos was providing no opportunity. Clearly he didn't feel the same way.

After a few hours, their skin encrusted with salt and a sunburn starting on her nose, Talia suggested they pack up. Sofia's face dropped but Talia could see her charge was flagging; they'd spent a lot of time out in the wind and sun.

Wordlessly Angelos helped to pack up and then took the picnic basket from her as they started back towards the villa. Talia had the pleasantly tired sensation of having had a full day out, although after suffering one of Angelos's frowning glances she realised she must look a complete mess.

Her hair was tangled and salty, hanging in damp ropes down her back, and her nose was probably Rudolph-red by now. She'd put her T-shirt and shorts back on over her swimsuit, which had made damp patches on the fabric. Yes, she was really rocking a sexy, seductive look right now. Not that she wanted Angelos to see her as sexy or seductive, of course. Not that he ever would, even if she wore a black lace bustier and fire-engine-red stilettos.

Now where had that image come from? Talia let out an incredulous little laugh as she pictured herself in such a ridiculous getup. She hated heels and the only thing she wore to bed was a very old, very large and very comfy T-shirt. This made her smother another laugh, and Angelos glanced at her, eyes narrowed.

'What's so funny?'

For a second she imagined telling him, and that made

her laughter cut off like a tap being turned off. Would he be appalled or incredulous or both? She knew Angelos Mena was way, way out of her league. 'Nothing,' she assured him. 'Nothing at all.'

# CHAPTER EIGHT

BY THE TIME they reached home, dark clouds were billowing up on the horizon and the wind that had been teasing and warm while they'd been on the beach had turned hard, buffeting them as they crested the hill above Angelos's villa.

'There will be a storm tonight,' Angelos remarked as he led the way down the hill towards the house. 'Make sure you close the shutters in your bedroom.'

'A storm?' Alarm prickled along Talia's skin at the thought.

Angelos must have heard the anxiety in her voice for he glanced at her, eyebrows raised. 'We will be perfectly safe in the villa. It is built to withstand such things.'

'I'm sure,' Talia murmured. She hated storms. Hated, hated, *hated* them. So much so that she had, in the past, swallowed a couple of sleeping pills while she waited one out. She'd rather be dead to the world than trembling in terror as it raged around her.

But she didn't want to knock herself out here, with Sofia needing her. Maybe the storm wouldn't be that bad. A little rain and wind was fine. It was the thunder and lightning that she couldn't stand, the booming that reverberated through her chest, the lightning that streaked through the sky and, for one blazing second, illuminated everything.

Just the thought of it made her head start to feel light, and a buzzing began in her ears. Talia took a deep breath, willing the panic away. She'd been so good, these last eleven days, in controlling her fear. Being on Kallos had felt, in a way, like being on the estate. Isolated. Safe.

*But a storm...*

'Talia?' Angelos asked, his voice harsh and insistent. 'Are you all right?'

'What?' She blinked up at him, swaying slightly where she stood. They'd walked down the hillside without her even realising it and they now stood on the terrace outside the kitchen. Sofia must have gone inside. 'I'm fine,' she said, even though she knew she wasn't. She dragged another deep breath into her lungs. 'Totally fine. Where's Sofia?'

'She went inside to change.' Angelos was still frowning at her, his gaze moving over her like a doctor checking for broken bones. 'Do you not like storms?'

'Not particularly.' The smile she gave him felt like a horrible rictus. The wind was picking up so much now her hair blew about her face, and then she heard a distant rumble and her heart free-fell towards her toes. 'I'll be fine,' she said as firmly as she could. She didn't want Angelos to see her anxiety, even though she knew she must be showing it, at least a little. She hated for anyone to know her weaknesses; it was bad enough for her grandfather and siblings to feel sorry for her, to know how damaged she was. She couldn't bear for others to see it, and especially someone like Angelos, who was so strong and capable. He probably wasn't afraid of anything.

'If you're sure,' he said, sounding doubtful, and Talia forced a nod.

'I'm sure.'

She walked up to her bedroom and ran a shower, glad

that the rush of water drowned out the noise of the thunder rumbling in the distance, like a discontented giant. She rested her head against the tile as she let the water stream over her and tried to calm the racing of her heart.

*It's just a storm. It can't hurt you. No one can hurt you now. You're safe. You're safe.*

Words she'd repeated to herself countless times over the last seven years, but she never really believed them, not deep down. She'd never trusted that she would be safe, not unless she was hidden behind high walls, locked gates, like some frightened Rapunzel up in her tower.

*You're on an island. No one can hurt you here. No one can get to you.*

Really, she was so much safer on Kallos than anywhere else. She had to believe that, because if she didn't, she'd start thinking about how small the island was, how confined and cut off. And then her claustrophobia would kick in, and she'd *really* be in trouble.

Resolutely Talia turned off the shower and dressed in her one pair of jeans and a thick fleece. With the approaching storm the weather had cooled down and she stood by the window for a moment, gazing out at a wide sky the colour of a livid bruise before she closed and latched the shutters, releasing a shaky breath. She still had dinner to get through.

Downstairs the house was dark, the shutters all closed against the storm. Somewhere in the distance a loose shutter banged, and the sound made unease prickle along Talia's scalp. She hated that lonely, mournful sound. She shivered, and then jumped when she heard Angelos's low voice coming from right behind her.

'Are you cold?'

'No…' She turned, blinking in the gloom to see him emerge from his study. His hair was damp from a shower and he'd changed into faded jeans that moulded to his thighs and a grey crew-neck sweater that clung to his chest. Even in the midst of her panic Talia couldn't keep from feeling a kick of desire at the sight of him. He was glorious, utterly and wonderfully male.

'You shivered,' Angelos explained, coming closer so she breathed in the scent of his skin, warm male and soap. Her mind spun crazily. 'So I thought you were cold.'

'I'm fine.' She took a needed step backwards. If he came any closer she'd start purring. 'Shall we go into the kitchen?' She turned away without waiting for a reply, her heart bumping in her chest both from Angelos's closeness and the storm outside. Did Angelos realise the effect he had on her? She had a feeling she might as well have her attraction to him spelled out in blazing letters on a neon sign, but even so she hoped he didn't notice.

In any case, he was probably used to women lighting up like a firework when he was around. Maria had mentioned the other nannies trying to get into his bed, after all. Angelos probably found her obvious desire amusing and a little pitiful, which of course it was.

She had to get a handle on it, as well as on her panic. *Control.* That was what was needed here. Deep, even breathing to steady her heart rate, and a logical reminder that she really was safe.

Taking a deep breath, Talia joined Maria and Sofia at the table. The kitchen was warm and brightly lit, the spicy smell of roasted lamb filling the air, and all of it helped to push back her anxiety about the storm.

Then Angelos came into the room and her stomach flip-flopped at the nearness of him. She was a *mess.*

Talia ate her dinner as quickly as she could without being rude, and then chivvied Sofia upstairs to get ready for bed without waiting for coffee. Angelos looked bemused, but since he'd been the first to leave the table last night Talia didn't think he could complain.

She stood by the window while Sofia readied for bed, listening to the rain sleet against the shutters. It sounded like a herd of elephants had taken residence on the roof, but the noise didn't bother her. She could handle rain.

Then a distant rumbling sounded, followed by the ear-splitting crack of thunder. Talia let out a little shriek, clutching at the wall to balance herself, and Sofia came out of the bathroom, toothbrush in hand, a frown on her face.

'Okay?' she asked, and Talia nodded quickly.

'Yes, I'm okay.' Maybe if she kept saying it, it would actually become true.

She read Sofia a chapter from the English book they both enjoyed, although Talia didn't know how much the girl understood. Then she kissed her goodnight and hurried to her own bedroom, where she prayed she could shut out this awful storm.

Two hours later Talia was contemplating taking the sleeping pills. She lay on her bed, a pillow clutched to her stomach, her body drenched in icy sweat as the storm swirled and raged around the house. The lightning was coming every thirty seconds or so, a savage crack and then a blinding light that lit up the room like a disco and made Talia whimper as memories streaked through her.

Cowering in the corner, her arms wrapped around herself, wondering if this would be her last night on earth. The rain thundering on the tin roof over her, the thunder shaking the shed's flimsy sides, the sound of raised voices right outside the door, and then the door *opening...*

She whimpered again and closed her eyes, her whole body trembling with a terror as elemental as the storm outside.

She could take a shower again, and let the noise drown

out the sounds of the storm, but at this point Talia wasn't sure she could get off her bed. She felt paralyzed by her own fear, her mind a terrible blank, and it took all her strength simply to lie there and survive. Surely it would be over soon. Surely this nightmare would end…

*Just as it had ended before.* She tried to cling to that, to the memory of her salvation, but the thunder boomed again and lightning streaked through the cracks in the shutters and all she could think about, all she could feel, was the icy, overwhelming terror at being locked in a tiny room while the storm raged ahead and her life hung by a single, precarious thread.

Angelos closed his laptop, unable to concentrate on work with the storm raging outside. Although if he were honest, it wasn't the rain and wind outside that was distracting him; it was the storm inside himself.

He'd been feeling restless and uneasy all day, ever since he'd gone on the picnic with Talia and Sofia. Ever since he'd told Talia a little bit about his childhood, cracked open the firmly closed door to his soul. And, he admitted reluctantly, ever since he'd felt her soft, pliant body against his, had seen her breasts rise and fall with agitated breaths, had absorbed the impact of the desire lighting those golden-green eyes…

Groaning, Angelos rose from his desk. No more work tonight. He'd settle for a cold shower and a sleepless night, and perhaps tomorrow he would return to Athens.

Except he didn't want to go to Athens. Despite the restlessness surging through him, he'd enjoyed his time with Sofia today.

*And Talia. You enjoyed your time with her too.*

For Sofia's sake he would stay. It was her birthday in a few days and he tried to be present for that at least. Tried to be the kind of father he knew he never really could be, not when it had mattered.

Angelos headed upstairs, the house dark all around him, the beams and shutters creaking from the force of the wind. He'd just crossed the landing when he heard a sound he first mistook for the wind, a low moaning. He stilled, frowning, and then he heard it again. An animal sound, one of pain or fear.

Frowning, Angelos went down the hallway, his heart rate kicking up at the thought that Sofia might be distressed by the storm. Then he recognised the sound was not coming from his daughter's room at the end of the hall, but from behind the closed door right in front of him. Talia's room.

Again he heard the moan. 'Talia?' he called softly, knocking on the door. No answer. Angelos cocked his head, his brow furrowed as he strained to hear. All was silent, but unease prickled along his spine. What if Talia was ill? She'd been terribly quiet at dinner, but Angelos had put it down to all the sun and sea, plus the fact that she didn't like storms. She'd still been attentive and loving to Sofia, and he hadn't been able to fault her. He'd just been sorry when she'd gone, as if a light had left the room, energy draining from it.

He heard the moaning again and, rapping sharply first, Angelos opened the door.

He stopped on the threshold, appalled at the sight before him. Talia was curled in a foetal position on the bed, a pillow clutched to her chest. Her hair was damp with sweat, her face sickly white with a greenish tinge.

Angelos swore under his breath before he strode towards her. 'Talia, what has happened, are you ill…?'

She barely seemed aware of him as he crouched next to her and peered anxiously into her face. He touched his hand to her forehead, sucking in a hard breath as his palm came in contact with the iciness of her skin. He'd been expecting her to be hot with fever, but she was terribly, terrifyingly cold.

'Talia…' he murmured, and brushed her damp hair away from her forehead. She barely looked at him, her eyes glassy, her gaze unfocused. Her whole body was rigid.

Realisation slammed into Angelos with breathless force. She wasn't ill; she was *scared*. Utterly and completely terrified. He'd seen how she'd been nervous about the storm, but he'd had no idea she had a full-fledged phobia.

'Talia, it's all right,' he murmured as he continued to stroke her damp hair away from her face. She didn't look at him, hardly seemed aware of him. 'It's all right,' he said again, uselessly, because he could see that it wasn't all right at all.

A shudder ran through her body, wracking her slender frame, and her eyes closed in what seemed like surrender to the fear that gripped her.

'Come on,' Angelos said, and he put one arm around her shoulders, sliding the other under her body. 'Let's get you cleaned up at least.' She was incredibly light and fragile in his arms, even as a dead weight, although after a few seconds she curled into him, resting her cheek against his chest, her legs tucked up, her arms around his neck.

Angelos's heart stumbled and for a moment he just stood there, conscious of the closeness of her, the way she trusted him completely.

Then he moved into the en-suite bathroom, reaching out with one hand to turn on the shower before he gently put her back down on her feet, supporting her with one arm.

'Can you undress?' he asked, and she just looked at him, her eyes still wide and glassily blank.

He hesitated only for a second before he stripped the roomy T-shirt and men's boxers she'd been wearing as pyjamas from her body. He kept his movements efficient yet gentle, but even so he couldn't keep his insides from tightening at the sight of her body, golden, lithe and perfect. Small, high breasts sprinkled with freckles. A tiny waist and endless legs. He jerked his gaze back up to her face, ashamed that he'd been staring, but she wasn't even looking at him. Her whole body had started to tremble, her teeth chattering.

'Come on,' Angelos said, and helped her into the shower. She stood under the warm spray, her eyes closed, and then she leaned against the shower wall and slowly sank to the floor, her legs crumpling underneath her.

Muttering a curse Angelos went to her, mindless of the water that streamed over his clothed body, and pulled her into his arms.

She clung to him, her naked body curling into his, and after a while—Angelos didn't know how long—she stopped trembling.

Eventually she came to, like someone coming out of a trance. She moved away from him, water streaming down her naked body and slicking back her hair, appalled realisation swamping her eyes.

She opened her mouth but no words come out and Angelos knew she was beyond embarrassed. And yet he was not, even though he'd been sitting in the shower fully dressed, cradling a naked woman, for the better part of an hour.

Calmly he reached up and turned off the taps. The bathroom was plunged suddenly into steamy silence; Angelos rose, conscious of the way his shirt stuck to his body and his hair was plastered to his head.

'Let me get you a towel,' he said. Talia didn't answer.

He reached for one of the big fluffy towels piled on a shelf and she rose from the shower on unsteady legs, one arm braced against the wall as she stepped out of the shower.

'I…' she began, her voice wobbling all over the place.

'Don't,' Angelos said. Gently he wrapped her in the towel, covering her nakedness. 'Don't be embarrassed, I mean,' he clarified. Her face was fiery, and not just, he knew, from the heat and steam of the shower. She'd ducked her head low so she didn't have to look at him.

'How can I not be?' she returned in a suffocated whisper. She closed her eyes and a single tear squeezed out, trickling down her cheek.

'Talia…' Angelos's heart constricted with unfamiliar emotion as he wiped it away with his thumb. 'I'm sorry I didn't realise how storms affected you.'

'How could you know?' Her eyes were still closed, and another tear snaked down her cheek.

'Oh, Talia.' Without thinking Angelos gathered her up in his arms and carried her into the bedroom. He laid her down gently on the bed and she stared up at him, clutching the towel to her.

'You're soaked.'

He glanced down at his drenched clothes. 'And dripping onto your floor.'

'I don't mind.'

'I should go change.' He saw, to his gratification, a flicker of disappointment pass across her face like a shadow. 'I'll come back,' he promised. 'To check on you.'

She nodded and reluctantly he left the room. Back in his bedroom Angelos peeled off his damp clothes, wondering at his audacity at stripping his nanny naked, cradling her in the shower—what had he been *thinking*? But he hadn't been. He'd simply been reacting to her pain and need, and also to his own.

It had felt amazingly good to hold a woman after so long. To comfort a woman, to be the person she needed in a crisis. He'd needed to be needed. He'd craved being the comforter and protector, being *enough*.

Was it wrong of him, to have taken advantage of her pain to soothe his own?

But no, he'd helped her, or at least he hoped he had. And she'd helped him.

He pulled on a pair of loose pyjama trousers and a T-shirt, clothes he didn't normally wear since he preferred to sleep in a pair of boxer shorts or nothing at all. Then, combing his fingers through his damp hair, he went back to check on Talia.

In his absence she'd taken the opportunity to change into another billowy T-shirt and shorts, and she'd brushed her hair so it curled about her face in damp tendrils. She was sitting on her bed, her knees brought up to her chest, her eyes huge in her face. In the distance thunder rumbled.

Angelos sat on the edge of the bed. 'The storm's moving off now, I think,' he said quietly.

'Yes.' She nodded jerkily, her chin bumping the tops of her knees.

'Do you want to talk about it?' he asked, and she let out a shaky laugh.

'Not particularly.' The thunder rumbled again, and lightning flashed briefly, barely lighting the room, but it was enough to have Talia tensing again.

'You don't have to talk, if you don't want to,' Angelos said. God knew he had a few secrets himself. He glanced at the shuttered window. 'Are you going to be okay?'

She nodded again. 'I'm fine.'

'You don't sound fine,' Angelos said.

'It's okay…'

But it wasn't okay. Even though the storm was moving

away from Kallos, Talia still looked frightened. And Angelos didn't want to leave her alone. He *wouldn't* leave her alone, refused to leave anyone who needed him.

*Except Sofia. You left Sofia.*

But his daughter was better without him. At least, he'd thought she was, until Talia had started showing him otherwise.

'Move over,' he said, and her eyes widened, her spine straightening as she looked at him.

'What...?'

He nudged her leg with his own, and then gently took her by the shoulders and moved her to the side of the bed. He stretched out alongside her, smiling a bit at her obvious surprise. 'I'll stay,' he said. 'Until the storm ends completely.' And then, because it felt so natural and he couldn't keep himself from it even if he had wanted to, he took her into his arms.

Talia remained rigid in his embrace for a few seconds, and then, just as she had before, she relaxed into him, her body softening against his as she let out a breathy little sigh of contentment.

Angelos rested his chin on top of her head, enjoying the feel of her in his arms, the simple closeness of another person. She smelled like almonds and she was so warm and soft and slender. His libido stirred insistently; it was impossible not to imagine sliding his hands under her voluminous T-shirt, feeling her warm, satiny skin under his palms as he cupped the small, perfect breasts he'd seen earlier, kissed each freckle...

As surreptitiously as he could Angelos shifted slightly away from Talia. The last thing she needed right now was to feel the hard evidence of his arousal. It was, he acknowledged wryly, going to be a long night.

# CHAPTER NINE

TALIA WOKE TO sunlight and an empty bed. She blinked the world into focus, her heart giving a funny little dip at the sight of the smooth expanse of sheet next to her. At some point in the night, and she had no idea when, Angelos had left her.

Talia flipped onto her back and stared up at the ceiling as memories of last night unspooled through her mind like scenes from a movie. Angelos coming in and seeing her drenched with sweat and shaking with terror. Angelos gently removing her clothes, stepping into the shower with her, holding in his arms.

And she'd let him. Of course she'd let him. She'd never felt so treasured, so *protected*, and it had been the most amazing and incredible feeling in the world. It had felt deeper and more important than any physical desire that she'd felt for him, although there had been that last night too.

Resting her cheek against his chest, hearing the steady thud of his heart as he cradled her...she'd been so tempted to tilt her head upwards and let him kiss her.

But of course he probably *wouldn't* have kissed her. He'd been wonderfully kind last night, comforting her when she'd been in the grip of a major panic attack, but that's all it had been. Comfort.

And for what he'd done, Talia knew, he deserved an explanation. One she didn't relish giving, because she hated for anyone to pity her, to know her weakness. But Angelos had already seen her weakness, so perhaps she had nothing left to lose.

Sighing she rose from the bed and went to get dressed. Sofia was just finishing her breakfast as Talia came into the kitchen, instinctively glancing around for Angelos. She didn't know whether to feel relieved or disappointed when she saw he wasn't there, but she caught Maria noticing her wandering gaze and a blush rose to her cheeks. Maria's lips pursed. The housekeeper didn't miss *anything*.

'Hey, Sofia,' Talia said brightly, and avoiding Maria's speculative gaze, she sat down at the table and helped herself to fresh fruit.

After breakfast Sofia went off with Ava for her lessons, and resolutely Talia went in search of Angelos. She found him, predictably, in his study, and his terse, 'Enter,' when she knocked on the door made her wonder if last night had happened at all.

Then she opened the door and saw him sitting at his desk, dressed in his usual button-down shirt and pressed trousers, seeming brisk and remote and yet so utterly wonderful, and colour flared into her face.

To her surprise an answering colour touched Angelos's sharp cheekbones as he looked up at her. He cleared his throat and then closed his laptop. 'How are you feeling this morning?'

'I'm fine. Good actually.' She closed the door behind her and took a deep breath. 'I'm sorry for being so...' Her mind spun as she tried to think of a word for what she'd been.

'Don't be sorry, Talia,' Angelos filled in quietly. 'I'm

the one who should be sorry, for not realising how the storm affected you. I would have checked on you, if I'd known.'

'There was nothing you could have done. That is...' She swallowed convulsively, resisting the urge to press her hands to her hot face. 'Besides what you did. Which was wonderful and way beyond the call of...'

'Duty?' he supplied, quirking an eyebrow, amusement lighting his eyes, turning them almost golden, and making her insides fizz in response. Scowling the man was almost unbearably attractive. Smiling he was impossible to resist.

'Yes,' she managed, dragging her gaze away from his. 'I suppose.'

'I said last night and I will say it again, there is no need to feel embarrassed.'

'You don't think?' Talia blurted. 'You saw me *naked*. Not to mention sweaty and shaking and...' She closed her eyes briefly. 'I'd really rather not remember.'

His mouth twitched in what she thought was amusement. 'I've seen women naked before, Talia.'

'Like most of your nannies?' Angelos's eyebrows snapped together and, horrified, Talia slapped a hand over her mouth. 'I mean,' she said through her fingers, 'Maria mentioned that they've tried to seduce you. And failed.'

'Maria talks too much,' he replied, but he didn't sound angry.

Slowly Talia dropped her hand, knotted her fingers together. 'It's just I don't want you to think...' What? That her sweating and shaking was supposed to have been a turn-on? She was absolutely no good at this, Talia thought as a fresh wave of mortification swept over her. She had absolutely no experience with sex, or even talking about sex, and especially not with a man as gorgeous as Angelos Mena.

'I don't think that, Talia,' Angelos said. 'Last night you were in no shape for a seduction.'

'Right. Sorry.' She gave a little shake of her head. 'I'm handling this really badly. I actually came in here to thank you, and also to explain why I reacted the way I did last night. Because, contrary to what you may think now, I'm not actually scared of storms.'

Angelos's look was one of almost comical disbelief. 'You could have fooled me last night.'

'I know.' She gave a shaky laugh. 'Would you believe I actually liked storms when I was little? I loved watching them from the window of my bedroom, especially in summer. They were so…wild.'

Briefly, so briefly she almost missed it, something flared in Angelos's eyes. She felt a kick in her stomach and she forced herself to continue, to ignore the helpless desire this man so easily ignited in her, simply by saying a word. *Wild.* What would it be like, if Angelos let go of his tightly held control? Images flared in her mind, vague swirling pictures of limbs tangling, mouths pressing, hands reaching. She shoved them away and met Angelos's gaze. 'It's not the storm I'm scared of,' she explained. 'It's what it makes me remember.'

Angelos stilled, his hands resting flat on his desk. 'You don't have to tell me—'

'I know. But after what you did, how you helped me, you deserve to know.' And actually, she realised, she *wanted* to tell him—even though she'd tried to keep the whole awful episode hidden from everyone, just as her grandfather had kept it out of the press, both of them pretending it had never happened, because that was easier. She wanted someone to know, someone who, amazingly, might understand a little. She drew a deep breath, let the air fill her lungs and buoy her courage. 'When I was eighteen,' she stated, 'I was kidnapped.'

Angelos opened his mouth, but no words came out. 'Kidnapped...' he finally said, and his voice sounded hoarse, his tone horrified.

'I was travelling in Europe, after my high school graduation. It was meant to be my big exciting summer, exploring the world, having endless adventures. I was with a couple of friends...we took precautions and we didn't do anything stupid...' Even now she felt the need to justify herself, to explain how it wasn't her fault, because for years she'd tormented herself with the what-ifs. What if she'd been more careful? What if she'd travelled with more people? What if she could have done something to keep the disaster from unfolding the way it had?

Angelos had recovered himself and was now looking at her with his familiar hard stare, his eyes dangerously dark. 'What happened exactly?'

'We were in Paris. The City of Love.' She let out a short, sharp laugh and shook her head. 'Right in front of the Eiffel Tower. It felt like it should have been the safest place in the world. My friend Anna had gone to see about tickets to go up the tower and I was just taking a photo.' She felt her chest start to go tight, her throat constrict, as memories assailed her, memories she'd kept locked tightly away. 'I'd raised the camera up to my face, and was looking through the lens when...' She stopped, closing her eyes. That moment when her world had shifted, shattered. One second was all it had taken to go from carefree insouciance to utter, incredulous terror.

'Talia,' Angelos said in a low voice. 'You don't have to—'

'No, I want to,' she insisted. 'I do. I never talk about this, but I want to now...after what you did...'

'It wasn't that much—'

'It was, Angelos,' she responded, and she heard how her voice throbbed with sincerity. She saw something flash across Angelos's face and she realised he'd never given permission to call him by his first name. 'Sorry, should I not have…'

'Not have what?'

'Called you Angelos,' she muttered. Angelos let out a wryly disbelieving laugh.

'After everything, Talia, I think you can call me Angelos. In fact, I think it would be strange if you didn't.'

*After everything.* Two little words that made her remember how he'd held her so tenderly, how hard and solid his chest had felt beneath her cheek. How she'd wanted to stay there for ever, wrapped in his arms, protected and safe.

Angelos rose from behind his desk, and taking her by the hand, he drew her to the two club chairs in front of the fireplace. She sank onto one, her legs shaky, and he sat in the other. 'So they took you from the Eiffel Tower,' he prompted, his voice low and steady.

'They grabbed me so quickly. I didn't even see…' She swallowed hard, remembering how brutally and ruthlessly efficient the man had been, pulling her tightly to him, leaning down as if he were whispering in her ear, looking all for the world as if they were two lovers sharing an intimate moment. In reality he'd been pressing a chloroform-soaked cloth to her mouth and nose. She'd been unconscious in seconds.

She forced herself to meet Angelos's gaze and continue. 'They drugged me. When I woke up, I was in some kind of shed. It was locked, of course, and there was nothing in there. A dirt floor, a tin ceiling…barely room to stand up. And it was so dark.' A shudder ran through her. 'I had no idea where I was, or what they were going to do to me.'

Angelos's face was pale, his eyes like burning dark coals. 'That must have been utterly terrifying.'

'It was.' She pressed her lips together, memory rising inside her, choking her. 'A man brought me food and water, although he never spoke to me. After a while I actually started to feel bored, which sounds ridiculous, but I just wanted something to *happen*.' She shook her head. 'I was so naïve.' She lapsed into silence, remembering the endless days and weeks of sitting in that cramped cabin, filthy, exhausted, emotionally spent. Almost wanting it to be over…for good. She knew what despair felt like. She understood hopelessness.

'What happened then, Talia?'

She jerked her gaze up, refocusing on Angelos. 'There was a storm one night. A terrible storm, worse than the one we had here. I think the lightning must have struck something nearby, because there was a terrific crash, and I heard something fall nearby, a tree, I suppose. I was afraid they would leave me to die in there and save themselves. Or maybe they'd died, and no one would ever find me.' Her fists had become bloody and bruised from banging on the door, a useless but instinctive bid for freedom.

'But they didn't?' he prompted quietly when she'd fallen into silence once more.

'No, they didn't. In the middle of the storm the door opened and there were several men, some I hadn't seen before. I couldn't see their faces…they dragged me out of the room. I had no idea what was going to happen. One of them had a knife.' She stopped, expelling a trembling breath, and heard Angelos mutter a curse. 'They didn't actually hurt me,' she said. 'They held a knife to my throat, but it was only for a picture. A ransom note. I didn't realise that at the time though. I couldn't think about anything. I could barely stand up.' She tried to smile ruefully but her facial muscles felt like they weren't working properly. 'They took the photo, and then they pushed me around a bit, and then they shoved me back in the shed.'

'I cannot imagine, Talia,' Angelos said. He was gripping the armrests of his chair, his knuckles white, his face bloodless.

'They weren't as smart as they thought they were though,' Talia continued, trying to inject a cheerful note into her voice and failing. 'They sent the photo of me to my grandfather, and he used his resources to locate me from what they'd seen in the photo and then to prosecute the kidnappers. Just twenty-four hours after they sent the photograph a helicopter came with a SWAT team to rescue me.'

'A helicopter,' Angelos repeated after a pause. 'Is that why you are scared of helicopters?'

'Sort of. The sound reminds me of that whole time, and the rescue effort was…intense.' She remembered the shouts, the staccato gunfire, the stranger who yanked her arm so hard he nearly dislocated her shoulder as he pulled her towards the waiting helicopter. At that point she hadn't even known if the man was friend or foe, or if she was facing freedom or death. She'd collapsed inside the helicopter, watching in disbelief as a man was shot and killed right in front of her. And then the soul-freezing terror had morphed into an incredulous and numb relief, both emotions overwhelming.

'But really,' she told Angelos, 'any confined space is difficult. From…from being in that shed. I've tried some different therapies for it, but none of them have worked.' She gave him a lopsided smile. 'But I supposed claustrophobia and a fear of thunderstorms is a small price to pay for my freedom.'

Angelos shook his head, his hands still clenched on the armrests. 'I don't know how you survived such a thing.'

'How does anyone survive?' she answered. 'And *survive* is the right word, because sometimes it's felt as if that's all I'm doing.'

'What do you mean?'

'Coming to Athens was the first time I'd got on an airplane in seven years. The first time I used public transportation, or ventured out of my comfort zone at all. After the kidnapping I dropped out of college and retreated to my grandfather's estate. I couldn't face people, and just being in a small space, even in a classroom, sent me into a blind panic. My grandfather was understanding, and he let me hide myself away. I think he thought I'd come out again, but I never did.'

Confusion clouded Angelos's eyes and he shook his head. 'But you must have. You said you were an artist—'

'I have a private studio there. Clients come to me. I hardly ever leave. I can't stand crowds, or cities, or small spaces. Which leaves me feeling pretty limited sometimes, but I've been happy. At least, I thought I was happy.' But now, with a taste of what it felt like to truly live again, to feel excitement and happiness and desire, Talia knew she hadn't been. She'd been content, maybe, but that was all. She'd been living a half-life without realising it, telling herself it was enough.

'But you did come to Athens,' Angelos said. 'You *tried*. That's important, Talia.'

'Yes…' But he didn't know why she'd tried. Talia could tell that Angelos assumed she'd come to Greece simply to break out of her cocoon. Now would be the perfect time to tell him about the book, the real reason she was here.

And yet she stayed silent. She might have been brave in coming here, but in many ways she was still a coward. Because she didn't want to risk Angelos's anger at learning her true motives, feeling deceived. She didn't want to leave Kallos or Sofia. She didn't want to leave *him*.

The realisation of how much she was starting to care about this man drove her upright. 'I should go. Sofia's lessons will be finished, and we were going to sketch today, outside.'

Angelos rose also and reached for her hand. The slide of his fingers along hers was infinitely, achingly sweet, and it lit a flame of need in her belly. 'Thank you,' he said quietly. 'For telling me all of that.'

'Thank you,' Talia answered, 'for comforting me last night.'

And then, because she didn't trust herself not to throw herself into Angelos's arms just as she had last night, she yanked her hand away and hurried from the room.

# CHAPTER TEN

CONSIDERING EVERYTHING SHE'D confessed, everything that had *happened*, Talia expected to feel embarrassed and exposed. Yet sitting on the beach with Sofia, sketchpads on their laps, she found she wasn't squirming internally with humiliation at how much she'd revealed. She felt…free. At peace in a way she hadn't expected.

For the last seven years she hadn't talked about the kidnapping to anyone. She knew Giovanni blamed himself for the whole affair, because the men had kidnapped her for money, knowing her to be an heiress. But Giovanni had rescued her; it was he who had accessed satellite photos to identify where she was being held from the picture the kidnappers had sent. She'd never blamed Giovanni. He'd been her saviour. And she'd respected his desire to forget the whole episode…or at least act as if she had. Her siblings had followed suit.

But secretly, or not so secretly considering her phobias and isolation, the kidnapping had tormented her with its terrible memories. For years she'd suffered nightmares that left her shaking, and the tiniest things could set her off: the sound of a lock turning, the creak of a door. She'd tried therapy, but talking to a stranger had only made her feel more exposed and raw. She'd learned to avoid triggers and read up on PTSD and kept everything buried deep inside.

Until Angelos.

Amazing, how *validating* it had felt when he'd told her it must have been terrifying. To have him sympathise and understand without pity or judgement.

She wished she could do something in return, help him in some way, for she knew that Angelos must have his own dark memories, his closely guarded secrets. But despite the comfort he'd offered her last night, she knew they still didn't have the kind of relationship that would allow that conversation.

'Hello, you two.'

Talia stiffened in surprise, pleasure flooding through her as she saw Angelos strolling down the beach. Sofia's face lit up as Angelos came to stand in front of them, the wind off the sea ruffling his hair.

'How's the sketching?' he asked, and Talia nudged Sofia to show her father her work. Shyly she offered up the paper and Angelos took it and studied it carefully.

Talia couldn't understand the Greek he spoke to her, but even she basked in his smile. She loved that he was trying more with Sofia, and that it was working.

They spoke in Greek for a few moments and then he turned to Talia. 'It is Sofia's birthday in a few days—'

'Is it?' Talia interjected in surprise. She wagged a finger at Sofia, smiling. 'You should have told me.'

'Perhaps we can do something to celebrate,' Angelos said, and Talia felt as if her heart was a balloon expanding in her chest, full of hope. He almost sounded as if they were a family.

'Of course we must celebrate,' she said. She turned back to Sofia. 'What would you like to do?'

Timidly Sofia spoke in Greek to her father. Angelos listened, a frown furrowing his forehead, and the balloon inside Talia started to deflate. Why did he have to look so angry?

He spoke sharply back and Talia watched in dismay as Sofia nodded in acceptance, the light dimming from her eyes. She ducked her head so her hair slid in front of her face, hiding her scarred cheek, an action Talia had come to associate with Sofia's lack of confidence, and one she thankfully hadn't done for a while.

'What is it?' she burst out. 'Surely whatever Sofia wants to do, we can manage…' Sofia hardly seemed the type of girl to ask for something unreasonable.

'She wants to go sailing,' Angelos said tightly. 'To Naxos. I told her it was not possible.'

'Why?'

'Because she wants to go with you,' Angelos explained. 'I don't think you want to be on a small boat in the middle of the sea.'

*'Oh.'* For a moment all Talia could do was gape. He was thinking of her, and her fear of being confined. She was so surprised and touched that it took her a few seconds to gather her composure. She turned to Sofia with a smile. 'I think sailing sounds like a lot of fun.'

'Talia,' Angelos protested. 'You don't have to—'

'But I do,' she said quietly. 'It's Sofia's birthday. If this is how she wants to celebrate, then I want it too.' And she just wouldn't think about how long she'd be on a small boat. 'Besides,' she told Angelos with more conviction than she actually felt, 'it's not as bad as a helicopter. The sides are open, and we'll be out on the sea. It'll be fine.'

Angelos was still frowning. 'I don't like it,' he said, and Talia saw Sofia's hopeful smile slide off her face once more.

'It'll be fine,' she said again. She'd make sure it was.

She was still telling herself that three days later, as she

and Sofia stood on the beach while Angelos readied the sailboat. It was a very small boat, barely big enough for all three of them to sit in. Nerves coiled tightly in her belly and she tried to keep her fists from clenching. She could do this. It wasn't as if she had four walls bearing down on her. There was no reason to feel trapped.

Except once she was out on the water, she *would* be trapped. And Angelos had told her it would take an hour to sail to Naxos, which felt like an incredibly long time.

'Ready, Papa?' Sofia called. She was jumping up and down in her excitement and the sight of the little girl looking so happy was enough to calm Talia's fears for a moment. They'd started the day with a special birthday breakfast and Sofia had opened presents from everyone.

Talia hadn't known what to get for Sofia's birthday; she hadn't left Kallos since she'd arrived two weeks ago and she hadn't brought anything remotely suitable to give her as a present. In the end she'd painted Sofia a picture of the villa and the beach, remembering how Sofia had sketched it when they were back in Athens. The little girl had been incredibly pleased with the picture, and Talia had promised to look for a frame for it when they went to Naxos.

'All right, I think we're just about there,' Angelos called. He looked amazing and remarkably at ease, wearing board shorts and a T-shirt that the wind pressed to his well-muscled chest. Over the last few days he'd spent a fair amount of time with Sofia and Talia, coming in as soon as Sofia's lessons were finished. At first he'd merely watched and smiled as Talia and Sofia played a game or did some sketching, but in the last day or two he'd started, at Talia's gentle urging, to join in. It made her heart ache with bittersweet joy to see how clumsily yet sincerely Angelos tried with his daughter, how hard these simple interactions were for him, and yet he *tried*. And that, just as he'd told her, was important.

Now he extended a hand towards Sofia, and helped her to clamber into the boat. Once Sofia was seated he turned to Talia, who was still rooted on the shore, unable to keep from eyeing the boat nervously.

His eyebrows snapped together as he held out his hand. 'Are you all right?'

'Yes...' Her voice wavered and she tried to smile. 'It's just...it is a pretty small boat. I thought you'd have a yacht or something.'

'I do have a yacht,' Angelos answered. 'It's docked in Piraeus. Sofia prefers the sailboat.'

'Oh. Right.' Of course he had a yacht. No matter how humble his beginnings, Angelos was a millionaire now. He exuded power from every pore. Masculine power. Over the last few days Talia had tried to hide her attraction to Angelos, but at times she felt overwhelmed with the desire, the need, to touch him. To feel his heart beating against her cheek once more, to taste his lips...

At night she lay in bed, restless and aching, amazed at how many new desires this man had awoken in her. She'd never felt this way about anyone before, hadn't even known such strong feelings existed.

And Angelos, as far as she could tell, seemed utterly unmoved.

'Talia?' he prompted, and taking a deep breath, she reached for his hand. The feel of his fingers closing over hers was enough to send her heart rate skittering and she tried to hide how uneven her breathing was, but the flush to her face was unavoidable. Maybe Angelos would chalk it up to the sun, or maybe he knew she found him irresistible and was being polite by ignoring it.

He guided Talia to her seat by the tiller, one arm around

her shoulders, which only made it worse, and yet also wonderfully, achingly better. She loved it when he touched her. She just wished he'd touch her more.

'Everyone ready?' Angelos asked as Talia buckled her life vest. She managed a sunny smile and a nod.

'Totally.'

Angelos pushed out, and as the boat bobbed into the deeper waters, the wind caught and filled the sails.

It felt like flying. Talia had been out on a sailboat as a child, although not since the kidnapping, for the obvious reason. Now she knelt by the tiller, her face tilted to the wind and sun, enjoying the way the boat skimmed across the glinting water. She could hardly credit, but she was actually enjoying this, and it reminded her of how much she'd used to enjoy, how adventurous she'd been. Seven years ago she'd lost a big part of herself and it had taken coming to Greece to begin to find it again. It had taken her grandfather to push her gently. Without Giovanni, she never would have left the safety of the estate.

Thinking of her grandfather made Talia flinch inwardly with guilt. She'd emailed him several times over the course of the last few weeks, reassuring him she was looking for the book…which was a lie. Beyond looking in the villa's library, she hadn't done anything. She hadn't wanted to risk this fragile peace and happiness she'd found here, with Angelos.

*Who you are kidding? You don't have anything with him.*

Angelos was a powerful, attractive, worldly man. Who knew how many women he had in Athens, or indeed around the world? He'd never be interested in someone like her, who cringed at her own shadow, who had no experience in anything.

And in any case, in a month's time she'd never see him

again. She had no reason whatsoever not to ask about her grandfather's book.

Angelos had come to sit beside her, one hand on the tiller, the other shading his eyes from the sun. Sofia was on the other side of the small craft, gazing down at the shimmering water speeding by, the wake from the boat as white as whipped cream.

'Do you like poetry?' Talia blurted, and then winced inwardly at the abrupt absurdity of the question.

Angelos stared at her for a moment, bemused. 'Now where did that question come from?'

'I was just curious.' She bit her lip, misery and indecision swamping her. She knew of no good way to come clean to Angelos and admit why she'd come here in the first place. But maybe he wouldn't be angry. Maybe he'd understand. And even if he didn't, she knew she had to say something. She had to find a way to mention her grandfather's book.

'I can't say I'm particularly well-versed,' Angelos answered, 'if that isn't too terrible a pun.'

'I only wondered, because my grandfather mentioned a Mediterranean poet that he liked,' Talia said, and Angelos's forehead furrowed. Clearly he didn't see the connection, and that's because there wasn't one.

'Tell me about your grandfather. You speak about him quite a lot.'

'Do I? I suppose that's because he raised me.' Relief trickled through her at the realisation that Angelos was providing her with an out. 'He took over the raising of me and my brothers and sisters after my parents died.'

'How many brothers and sisters do you have?'

'Seven,' Talia answered, 'including my half-brother, Nate. Five brothers and two sisters.'

'That's a lot,' Angelos remarked. 'Are you close to all of them?'

'Mostly, in different ways, although I don't see Nate very much.' She frowned, thinking of the elusive half-brother who had always skirted the fringes of her family. 'My father had an affair, before I was born, and Nate was the result.' She grimaced. 'Which puts my parents in a bad light, I know. They were...weak people, I think. But I still missed them, the idea of them.'

'I suppose bad parents are better than none.'

'Do you think that? You didn't grow up with any parents...'

'No.' Angelos stared out at the sea, his mouth pressed into a firm line. 'I don't know. I suppose I would have preferred almost anyone to the care home, or scratching a living on the docks.'

Talia shook her head in genuine admiration. 'It's amazing, how far you've come.'

'Just luck,' Angelos dismissed with a shrug of his shoulders, as he had before.

'More than luck,' Talia insisted. 'Not many people could do what you have done, Angelos.'

A brief look of something close to anguish contorted Angelos's features and then he looked out to sea again. 'Maybe,' he allowed, 'but I've failed in other ways.'

Talia felt as if her heart was bumping its way up her throat. 'What do you mean?'

Angelos shook his head, and then nodded towards Sofia. 'This is her day. Let's not ruin it by talk of the past.'

Which made her even more intrigued, but Talia knew better than to press it. She turned to Sofia with a smile, and they spent the next few minutes chatting in a mixture of broken English and Greek, both of them managing to get their meaning across. Mostly.

Several times she sneaked a glance at Angelos; he was still staring out at the sea, his eyes narrowed against the sun, the set of his mouth seeming bleak, and Talia wondered if she'd ever get an opportunity to ask Angelos what he'd meant when he'd said he'd failed.

He didn't talk about the past. He certainly didn't mention his failures. But he had to Talia; he'd almost told her about the fire. The realisation made Angelos's shoulders tense and his chest go tight. He didn't want to relive that awful day, the worst day of his whole life. He'd put those memories in a box and slammed the lid shut, but for some reason getting to know Talia was prying it open again. And that was not a good thing.

What was it about this woman with her clear, hazel gaze and her impish smile and incredible bravery that got to him? That made him want to tell her things, just as she'd told him? She'd been so honest with him, and he admired that deeply. But he wasn't capable of it himself.

In any case, she was leaving in a month. He'd enjoyed these last few days, and he was grateful to Talia for helping him to reconnect, at least a little, with his daughter. But it wasn't as if he and Talia had any kind of *relationship*. In a matter of weeks he'd never see her again.

He glanced at Talia; she'd stopped chatting to Sofia and was sitting back, her hands in her lap, the wind blowing her hair into golden tangles about her face. Her incredibly pale face, and belatedly Angelos noticed how her fists were clenched, how she was starting to tremble.

He knew they shouldn't have gone in the boat.

'Talia.' He slid off his seat and reached for her hands; they were ice cold. She didn't even look at him. 'Talia,' he said again, his voice hard and insistent, and she blinked him back into focus.

'Sorry…' she whispered, and Angelos muttered a curse. 'You have nothing to be sorry about.'

'It's just…we can't see land any more…' Her teeth chattered and Angelos slid next to her, putting an arm around her shoulders. She leaned into him, closing her eyes.

'It's okay,' he murmured. 'It's going to be okay. We'll get to land, we'll be safe. I'll keep you safe.' The words echoed through him, a promise he meant utterly and yet feared was hollow. After all, he'd broken it before.

Sofia turned to look at them, her face going nearly as pale as Talia's as she took in her nanny's sickly expression.

'Talia…'

Talia gave her a weak, apologetic smile and silently Sofia slid her hand into hers. Angelos went back to the tiller, guiding them as quickly as he could towards the shore.

The boat sped swiftly over the water; he kept glancing at Talia, making sure she was okay. Her face was pale but she lifted her chin bravely and squeezed Sofia's hand.

'I'm okay, Sofia,' she told the girl. 'Don't worry, please.'

The realisation that even in the midst of her suffering and fear, Talia was able to comfort his daughter, *cared* enough to comfort her, made something expand painfully in Angelos's chest.

He turned away quickly, not trusting the expression on his face, and steered them on to Naxos.

# CHAPTER ELEVEN

As soon as the sailboat reached the jetty, Angelos leapt out and tethered it before turning to Talia, his arms outstretched. She fell into his embrace clumsily, because her legs were so shaky, and heat scorched her once pale face as her panic started to recede, replaced by an almost as awful embarrassment.

'You must think…' she muttered as she stepped away from him.

'I think you're very brave, to go on this boat for my daughter's sake,' Angelos murmured. His hands still rested on her shoulders, his palms warm through the thin fabric of her sundress. 'Thank you,' he added, and then he released her to help Sofia out of the boat.

His words whirled through her mind as they set up camp on the stretch of beach by the harbour, the sand soft and warm beneath her bare feet.

*'I think you're very brave.'* Did Angelos really mean that? She didn't feel brave. She felt like the worst wimp, unable to hack so much as an hour in a sailboat. What kind of sad sack wasn't able to manage that?

Talia had accepted her limitations for so long they had stopped bothering her. At least, she'd thought they had. But now that she was experiencing more of life, both with Sofia and Angelos, she was coming to realise how little she'd had these last seven years…and how much she still wanted.

They spent the morning on the beach and then walked into the town of Chora for lunch. As they approached the whitewashed buildings, colourful cafés with striped awnings and tables outside, Talia watched as Sofia seemed to shrink into herself. Her hair slid in front of her face, her shoulders hunched, her whole demeanour making Talia think the girl wanted to hide herself.

In the nearly two weeks since she'd been on Kallos, Talia had grown so used to Sofia's face, to her bright smile and beautiful eyes as well as the puckered, reddened flesh that covered her entire cheek. She'd stopped noticing it at all, and Sofia had been much less self-conscious. But now she saw the shyness and insecurity come back, and she could tell Angelos noticed it too. As his daughter hid behind a curtain of curly dark hair, Angelos's scowl deepened, a deep furrow carved between his straight eyebrows.

'Where shall we go?' Talia asked brightly. She was determined to rescue this day and keep it special and happy for Sofia's sake. It wasn't every day a girl turned nine, after all. In hesitant, clumsy Greek, she asked Sofia where she would like to eat.

'There,' Sofia said, pointing to a café at the end of the street, and they headed towards it.

'You have learned some Greek,' Angelos remarked as they took their seats at one of the tables outside.

'Ava has been teaching me. I did ask Maria to ask you—'

'Yes, I remember. I said yes. And I am pleased you have made the effort.' He smiled, his eyes crinkling up at the corners, and Talia just about melted into a pool of slushy sentimentality.

She'd known she'd be a sucker for Angelos's smile.

In fact, as they ordered their meals and enjoyed the sunshine, chatting in a mixture of English and Greek, she started daydreaming that they were actually a family. That Angelos actually loved her.

The realisation of what she was fantasising about had her jolting upright, nearly spilling her drink.

Angelos's smile disappeared as he took in her pale face and slack jaw. 'Are you all right?' he asked in a low voice. 'This isn't too much for you?'

'It's fine,' Talia assured him with a shaky smile. And actually it *was* fine. She, who avoided crowds and cities, was actually enjoying sitting in a restaurant like a normal person.

It was Sofia she had been concerned about, until her fantasies about Angelos had derailed her whole thought process. Did she really want him to *love* her?

Did she love him?

'Talia?' Angelos's voice was tight with tension as he frowned at her, clearly concerned.

'It's okay.' She rested her hand on his, and then snatched it back when just the slide of skin across skin sent sensation skittering through her nerve endings. 'I'm fine. Really.'

Yet thoughts continued to zing through her mind as they ate lunch and then wandered through the town's street market. Love was such a huge concept, and one she didn't have a lot of experience with. Not romantic love anyway.

*And you can't be in love with Angelos. You barely know him. A week together, a single night of comfort...*

Mindlessly she studied some fabric piled on a market stall, green silk shot through with gold thread. Angelos joined her, standing so close she could feel the heat of his body, inhaled the scent of his aftershave, and had to close her eyes against the wave of desire that crashed over her.

'You would look lovely in that,' he said, gesturing to the silk.

Talia's heart lurched alarmingly. 'Oh, I don't know…' she demurred. She had a crazy and near irresistible urge to lean against him, to have him wrap one strong arm around her.

*What was happening to her?*

'Why don't I buy some for a dress?' He spoke to the shopkeeper in Greek, who was more than happy to accommodate him.

'I don't need a dress…'

'You are wearing the only one you brought,' Angelos reminded her. 'And perhaps you will go somewhere special. Perhaps we all will.' He pointed to another fabric, this one bright pink. 'And that for Sofia,' he said, and addressed the shopkeeper again in Greek.

Impulsively Talia put a hand on his arm. 'Thank you,' she said softly, and Angelos turned to her, his mouth turning down in self-deprecation.

'It is only a bit of silk.'

'I don't mean that. I mean the way you are with Sofia.' She nodded towards the girl, who was inspecting some cloth dolls hanging from pegs on the other side of the stall. 'She is so pleased to have this time with you. I know it means a lot to her.'

Angelos shrugged, his gaze sliding away. 'It is very little.'

'Even so…'

'It is you I should thank, for making me realise she wants to spend time with me.'

'Why would you think she wouldn't?'

Angelos turned back to her, his gaze dark, his frown deepening. 'Because I disappointed her terribly. I have not been the father she wants or needs.'

'But you are, Angelos, because you *are* her father. No mattered what happened before—'

He shook his head, the movement abrupt, as he handed some euros to the shopkeeper and took the cut fabric, now wrapped in paper. 'We will not talk about this.'

Talia watched as he strode towards Sofia, and then showed her the fabric he bought. Her shy, answering smile lit up her whole face and made Talia ache. Why did Angelos think he wasn't a good father? Why had he virtually ignored his daughter for so long? She wanted to know the answers, but she doubted she'd get them from him.

By early evening they were all feeling pleasantly drowsy. As they walked back towards the boat, Angelos tapped his finger against Talia's nose.

'You're a bit burned.'

'Which means more freckles,' she answered with a playful grimace.

'I like your freckles,' Angelos replied, and while Talia gaped at him he turned back to say something to Sofia.

He liked her freckles? Was she crazy, thinking that Angelos might like *her*? She had no experience with flirting or romance or love. She had no idea how to gauge Angelos's feelings, or even her own. And yet his simple statement had sent bubbles of excitement racing through her, as if she'd just imbibed a bottle of champagne.

'Will you be all right on the journey back?' he asked in a low voice as he helped Sofia scramble into the sailboat.

'I think so.' She smiled at him, trying not to let her gaze rove helplessly over his rugged features as those bubbles fizzed and popped. He'd had a bit of sun too, and his skin was even more bronzed and beautiful, the sharp planes of his cheekbones and the golden brown of his eyes making her breathless. 'Actually, I'm amazed at how easy this whole day has been,' she confessed. 'I haven't wandered around a town like this, in the crowds, for years.'

'Since...?' Angelos asked, his eyes darkening, and she nodded.

'I couldn't stand crowds. But I didn't mind them today.' *Because I was with you. Because you made me feel safe and protected.* She swallowed down the words and smiled instead. 'Thank you.'

'I didn't have anything to do with it—'

'You did,' she asserted, and then, throwing caution to the winds, she explained, 'When you held me that night... it was the first time I'd felt truly safe, really protected, in seven years. It gave me a confidence, Angelos, that I never thought I'd have again. So you see, you did have something to do with it. And I thank you for that.'

She didn't dare look at him, afraid she'd revealed too much, and so she scrambled into the boat by herself and sat next to Sofia, her face hot.

The moon rose over the Aegean as the boat skimmed the placid, dark waters and the breeze cooled their sun-burned skin. Talia put her arm around Sofia while the girl dozed against her and Angelos sat down, one hand resting on the tiller. He nodded towards Sofia.

'It's been a big day for her.'

'A big day for all of us.'

'Yes.' He paused, and in the gathering twilight she couldn't see his face. 'I'm proud of you, Talia. For facing your fears. Not everyone has the courage to do so.'

'I said before, you're the one who helped me.' She was glad for the darkness that hid her blush. 'The truth is I didn't plan on facing them. It's being here and seeing how Sofia...' She paused, afraid this might be too sensitive a subject for Angelos.

'What about Sofia?' he asked.

'She reminds me of me,' Talia said softly. 'How I've been inside for so long. Hiding myself. Ashamed of who I am.'

She felt Angelos stiffen even though he was several feet away from her. Pain emanated from him, seeming to tauten the very air. 'You think Sofia is ashamed of herself?' he asked, his voice low and aching. 'Of...of her scar?'

'She's certainly self-conscious about it,' Talia said carefully. She didn't have the courage to add, *Especially when you're around.* 'Have you noticed the way she hides her cheek with her hair?'

'Of course I've noticed it.' Angelos pressed his lips together and looked away. 'But she has no reason to be ashamed. None at all. She is a beautiful girl, inside and out.'

'Maybe you should tell her so,' Talia suggested. 'I think she'd like to hear it.'

'I do tell her,' Angelos answered, and she wondered if he wrote as much in her letters. 'Let us not talk of this any more,' he added, his tone final, and Talia knew she would have to let it go.

Neither of them spoke as Kallos appeared on the horizon, the villa washed in moonlight. Angelos moored the boat and then carefully scooped Sofia up into his arms; in sleep she snuggled against her father, her scarred cheek resting against his chest.

Seeing him acting so tenderly with Sofia made a lump form in Talia's throat. This man had so much love to give, and yet he seemed determined to lock it all away.

Or was she simply being foolishly hopeful, to think such a thing? To think he could fall in love with her?

Because she knew she was falling in love with him, whether it made sense or not. She might be inexperienced, but even she could recognise the ache in her heart, the hope in her soul and the need that flooded her body, all of it overwhelming, undeniable. Silently she followed Angelos across the beach and up to the villa.

The house was quiet and dark as they entered, Maria having already gone to bed. Angelos went upstairs to put Sofia to bed and Talia followed slowly, reluctant to end what had been, on the whole, a wonderful day. She wondered if she'd pushed Angelos too hard. Would he retreat back into his brusque, businesslike shell tomorrow, and once again ignore her and Sofia? She hated the thought.

Sighing she turned to her bedroom, only to still when she heard Angelos's voice, soft and disembodied in the darkness, coming from down the upstairs hallway.

'Thank you, Talia.'

'For what?' She turned around, her heart bumping hard as she saw him standing in the darkened corridor. Moonlight streamed through the high windows, touching his hair with silver. She couldn't see the expression on his face, but she felt his sincerity.

'For making this day possible,' he said. 'For making me realise it was necessary. I do take your point, you know. Sofia needs me, even if I'm not…'

'Not what?' Talia prompted softly when he'd trailed off with a little shake of his head.

'Not the father I want to be. The father I should be.' He'd stepped closer to her, close enough that she could touch him if she simply reached out one hand. Her fingertips tingled with the need to do so, to feel his solid strength beneath her palm, to comfort him as well as herself.

'You've said that before, Angelos, and I don't understand it. I'm not sure I believe it. I know you love Sofia. Why can't you be the father you want to be? The father Sofia needs?'

'Too much has happened,' he murmured. 'Things that can't be forgiven.'

'Anything can be forgiven.'

'Do you really believe that?' His voice had sharpened. 'Could you forgive the men who kidnapped you?'

Talia blinked, startled. 'How can you compare yourself to those brutes?'

'You don't know me, Talia. You don't know what I've—'

'I do know you,' she interjected, her voice turning ragged with the force of her conviction. 'I've seen you these last few days, Angelos, and I *do* know you. I know you love Sofia. I know you can be the father she needs, the man I—' She stopped suddenly, horrified by what she'd been about to blurt. *The man I love.*

'The man you what?' Angelos asked. He took a step closer to her, heat and intent evident in his hard stare.

'The man I've—I've come to know,' Talia answered, stammering in her embarrassment and anxiety. 'I have come to know you these last few days, Angelos. And I... I like the man I know.' *And so much more than that.* But she'd admitted more than enough already.

'Talia...' Angelos's voice broke on her name, and then, before she could even process what was happening, he pulled her towards him, his hands hard on her shoulders as his mouth crashed down on hers.

It had been ten years since she'd been kissed, and then only a schoolboy's buss. She'd never been kissed like this, never felt every sense blaze to life, every nerve ending tingle with awareness, nearly painful in its intensity, as Angelos's mouth moved on hers and he pulled her tightly to him.

His hard contours collided against her softness, each point of contact creating an unbearably exquisite ache of longing as she tangled her hands in his hair and fit her mouth against his.

She was a clumsy, inexpert kisser, not sure what to do with her lips or tongue, only knowing that she wanted more of this. Of him.

She felt his hand slide down to cup her breast, his palm hot and hard through the thin material of her dress, and a gasp of surprise and delight escaped her.

That small sound of pleasure was enough to jolt Angelos out of his passion-fogged daze, for he dropped his hand and in one awful, abrupt movement tore his mouth from hers and stepped back.

'I'm sorry,' he said, his voice coming out in a ragged gasp.

'No…' Talia pressed one shaky hand to her buzzing lips as she tried to blink the world back into focus. 'Don't be sorry,' she whispered. 'It was wonderful.'

'I shouldn't have—'

'Why not?' she challenged. She felt frantic with the desperate need to feel and taste him again, and more importantly, not to have him withdraw from her, not just physically, but emotionally. Angelos didn't answer and she forced herself to ask the question again. 'Why not, Angelos?'

'Because you are my employee, and I was taking advantage of you,' he gritted out. 'It was not appropriate…'

'I don't care about appropriate,' she cried. She knew she sounded desperate and even pathetic but she didn't care. She wanted him. She *needed* him. 'I care about you,' she confessed, her voice dropping to a choked whisper, and surprise and something worse flashed across Angelos's face. He shook his head, the movement almost violent and terribly final.

'No, Talia,' he told her flatly. 'You don't.'

And without giving her a chance to reply, he turned and strode towards his bedroom.

Talia remained in the darkened hallway, her body still throbbing with the need Angelos had lit inside her. She heard his door close, a soft, final-sounding click, and then with a shuddering sigh she turned towards her own bedroom.

She peeled off her clothes in the dark, gasping as the simple movements made the ache of need flare up inside her. She wanted Angelos to be the one to undress her, to touch her in ways she'd never been touched but now felt as if she couldn't live without. His mouth on hers, his hands on her skin…

But he obviously didn't feel the same way, and she'd humiliated herself in practically begging him to keep kissing her. In telling him she cared.

Cringing at the memory, Talia curled up on her bed, her knees tucked to her chest, and tried to will herself to sleep. It seemed to take an age before she finally fell into an uneasy, restless doze, only to wake to sunlight streaming through the shutters and the staccato sound of a helicopter whirring in the distance.

# CHAPTER TWELVE

ANGELOS LEANED BACK against the seat in the helicopter and closed his eyes, forcing back the memories of last night, of Talia pressing herself against him, her mouth opening under his like the sweetest of flowers. It was better this way. It had to be.

'Sir?' The pilot's voice broke into his thoughts and he opened his eyes, blinking in the bright sunshine of a summer morning.

'Yes, Theo?'

Theo waved towards the tarmac surrounding the helipad, raising his voice over the loud whirring of the helicopter's propeller. 'There is a woman...'

Angelos leaned forward, stiffening in surprise at the sight of Talia, wearing nothing but one of her huge T-shirts and a pair of skimpy boy shorts, striding towards the helicopter, a look of fury on her face.

'Cut the engine,' Angelos said tersely. The last thing he wanted was for Talia to be hurt. The wind generated from the propeller's blades was whipping her hair about her face in golden tangles, and her T-shirt to her body so Angelos could see every perfect, slender contour—and so could his pilot.

A jealousy so primal and fierce it would have shocked him had he possessed the sangfroid to consider it rose up inside him, making him leap out of the helicopter and swallow the space between him and Talia in two giant steps.

'What the hell do you think you're doing?'

'What the hell do you think *you're* doing?' she challenged. Her eyes glittered with golden-green fury and she jutted her chin at a proud, stubborn angle. 'Running away?'

'I am returning to Athens,' Angelos bit out. 'For business.'

'Liar. Liar *and* coward.'

'How dare you insult me in such a way,' he snapped. 'I am your employer—'

'As you reminded me last night. You bring that one out whenever it suits you—'

'This is not the place for such a conversation. Anyone can see you are barely dressed.'

She arched an eyebrow, magnificent even in a pair of pyjamas. 'Anyone? I don't see a crowd of bystanders.'

'My pilot, Theo.' Angelos gestured to the helicopter. 'I don't particularly want him to see what—' He stopped, swallowing the words he'd been going to say. *What is mine.*

Talia wasn't his. Not remotely. And she never could be.

'Fine, I'll go back to the house. But only if you'll come with me.' She folded her arms, chin still tilted proudly. 'Will you?'

'Fine,' Angelos answered. And when they were back in the house he would make it abundantly clear that they had no relationship, and that her place in his household was only as his daughter's nanny. Clearly last night had given Talia the presumption to take liberties with her position.

Suppressing the urge to drape his jacket over her, he strode back to the villa as Talia followed.

'Go change,' he instructed as they came into the house. 'And then you will meet me in my study.'

He didn't so much as look at her as he slammed into his study. It was time to put things back the way they were. Last night had been a moment of weakness and need that he intended never to show again.

Five minutes later a knock sounded on the door, and before Angelos could bid enter, Talia came in. She was wearing a pair of shorts that showcased her long gold legs and a T-shirt that was positively skimpy. Angelos could see the high, small breasts that he'd touched last night and, irritated, he yanked his gaze away.

'Don't you have any suitable clothes?'

'I've been wearing these clothes since I arrived,' Talia answered. Her voice was even but he sensed the tension and anger underneath, cracks in her calm surface. 'Why are you harping on about my clothes anyway? They hardly matter—'

'What matters,' Angelos cut across her, 'is the appalling liberties you've taken in your position as nanny.'

'*What?*' The word was expelled in an incredulous rush of air, Talia's jaw slackening and her eyes going wide as she stared at him in angry shock.

Angelos stood behind his desk, one hand resting on the back of his chair. 'I made it clear when I hired you what your position was to be. To supervise my daughter—'

'Are you implying I have been *negligent* in my duties?' Talia asked, her eyes now narrowing to golden-green slits.

'I'm implying that you have allowed your relationship with my daughter to give you the presumption to take liberties with me—'

'*I* take liberties with you?' Talia gasped in outrage. 'Correct me if my memory is faulty, but you're the one who kissed me last night.'

Angelos felt heat rush into his face and he stiffened his stance. 'I am not talking about that. In that instance I was at fault and I can assure you it will never happen again. I'm talking about your position in my family, Miss Di Sione, and the way you think you can—'

'We're back to Miss Di Sione?' she interjected with a sharp laugh. 'You really do feel backed into a corner, don't you?'

'Don't be ridiculous.'

'I don't think I am.' She took a step towards him. 'What is this really about, Angelos? Why were you leaving this morning?'

'I have business in Athens.'

'Did you even say goodbye to Sofia?'

'That is none of your concern—'

'Yes, it is, because I'm the one taking care of her. Did you?' Her question rang through the room and Angelos met her accusing stare unflinchingly.

'I wrote her a letter, which suffices.'

'You really believe that?'

'It is not for you to question my actions.'

She shook her head slowly, disbelievingly. 'You're scared,' she stated, and he stared at her coldly.

'Scared? Of what?'

Too late he realised he shouldn't have asked the question. He should have shut down this conversation before it had begun. Talia had no right—

'Scared of getting close to people. To Sofia, to me—'

'A single kiss does not mean we're close,' he informed her, knowing he was hurting her—and that he was a liar.

'I'm not talking about the kiss,' Talia answered quietly. Her face was flushed and humiliation sparkled in her eyes but she still stood straight and tall, holding his gaze, and it made Angelos feel a reluctant admiration for her. She was proud and beautiful and, considering all she'd endured, so very strong.

He wasn't worthy of her, not remotely.

'I'm talking about the conversations we had yesterday,' she continued, her voice trembling slightly. 'The things you admitted to me about your childhood, and how you feel you aren't a good father to Sofia. You feel threatened because I know all that, and you're wishing you hadn't said those things.'

She was utterly right, and his sense of honour forced him to admit as much. 'I am wishing it,' he told her. 'I never should have allowed us to have such…a connection.'

'Why not?'

'Because nothing can happen between us.'

She took a deep breath as she held his stare. 'Why not?'

He stared at her, flummoxed by her tenacity. 'Why not? Because…because it is simply not possible.'

'Do I have to say it again?'

'Why not?' he filled in for her, irritation creeping into his voice. 'Are you a glutton for punishment, Talia? Do you want me to spell it out for you?'

'I don't consider myself a glutton for punishment,' she answered, her voice wobbling a little, 'but yes, I do. Tell me why—why there couldn't be anything between us. I think we like each other…' Her face was fiery and she looked away for a few seconds, blinking rapidly, before she swung her gaze resolutely back to his.

'Because I am not interested in a romantic relationship with you,' Angelos informed her shortly. 'I have my daughter to consider—'

'I don't think Sofia would mind—'

'And my business,' he cut across her. 'In any case, you are American, and will be leaving here in a few short weeks. This whole conversation is the height of absurdity.'

He swung away from her, discomfited by how tempted he was to take her up on her blatant offer. He desired her, God knew; in the last seven years his libido had been like a dormant volcano that was now bubbling hotly to life. He wanted her very badly indeed.

And even more alarmingly, he *liked* her. He liked her sense of humour and her gentleness with Sofia, her understanding and her courage and her kindness.

He liked her so much that he couldn't stand the thought of her knowing how he'd disappointed the people he loved in the worst way possible. He couldn't stand the thought of her walking away from him.

'You are here,' he told her in a cold voice, his back still to her, 'as Sofia's nanny. That is all. Any…illusion of intimacy that occurred between us is simply that. An illusion. And you would do best to forget it ever happened.'

The silence after this pronouncement was awful, endless. Angelos could hear Talia's soft breathing; the gentle, hitched breaths reminding him of a hurt animal, of someone in pain.

'Very well,' she said at last. 'I will accept what you've said. I can hardly do otherwise. But I would ask, for Sofia's sake, that you not leave Kallos just yet. It was her birthday only yesterday, and she treasures this time with you. For her sake, will you stay? I will keep myself out of the way when the two of you are together. But just…' Her voice broke and Angelos closed his eyes, a shudder of pain ripping through him. 'Don't leave yet. Please.'

A long moment passed as Angelos mastered his composure. 'Fine,' he said, his voice toneless. 'But I do need to return to Athens. But I'll stay for a few more days. For Sofia's sake.'

'Thank you,' Talia said softly, and then he heard the door open and click softly shut as she left the room.

\* \* \*

She was so stupid. Slowly Talia walked upstairs, barricading herself in her bedroom as the realisation of how utterly she'd revealed and humiliated herself reverberated through her. She was so painfully, horribly stupid, to think Angelos cared about her. To demand he give a fledgling relationship between them a chance, when he obviously had no interest or intention of doing so. *I think we like each other.* What was she, in seventh grade?

She leaned against the door and slid slowly to the floor, cradling her head in her hands. *Stupid, stupid Talia. The first time you get a taste of life and love and you go crazy.* At least she was wiser now. Next time, if there was a next time, she'd know not to go begging. She'd wait for a man to show her he cared for more than just a kiss, amazing as it had been.

She heard Sofia go downstairs for breakfast, and then Angelos's low, murmured greeting as he came out of the study. At least he'd said he would stay. If she left Kallos in a few weeks having helped to strengthen the relationship between Angelos and his daughter, she would be happy.

Almost.

The day dragged, with Talia both hopeful and afraid of seeing Angelos around the house. He closeted himself in his study, and after lunch she took Sofia swimming. They splashed around in the water for a while, enjoying the sun, joking in their strange yet workable mixture of English and Greek.

'Sofia,' Talia asked when they were lying on the beach, the salt drying on their skin, 'did you like being on Naxos?'

Sofia turned to look at her in surprise. *'Ne...'*

'Would you like to go to school there? I saw there was a school in Chora. It's not so far in a boat, and you could have friends, then, besides us boring old grown-ups.'

Sofia frowned, trying to make out Talia's meaning, and so she explained it more clearly. 'School,' she said. '*Scholeio*? In Chora?'

Understanding brightened Sofia's face before it fell and she shook her head. 'Papa *ohi*,' she said. 'No.'

'Papa said no?'

'He not...want.' She shrugged, and Talia nodded in understanding.

'You think your father doesn't want you to go to school in Chora,' she surmised, and after a brief pause Sofia touched her scarred cheek, her fingers brushing the ridged flesh as she gazed at Talia with wide, sorrow-filled eyes. 'Because of that?' Talia exclaimed in surprise and dismay. 'Sofia, no. *Ohi*. Your papa doesn't care about that.'

But Sofia just shook her head and looked away.

The conversation lingered with her for the rest of the day, and after a sleepless night Talia decided she would have to confront Angelos about this latest revelation. She knew he would not take kindly to her interference, and worse, she was afraid the idea that Sofia thought he wanted her to hide away because of her scar would hurt him. But he had to realise how his behaviour was affecting his daughter.

It took three more days before she was finally able to find a moment alone with Angelos. He'd gone off the island for an overnight; Maria had said he was having a quick trip to Athens before returning, an explanation that satisfied Talia as she suspected previously he would have gone for weeks.

When he came back he spent his time with Sofia and she tried to make herself scarce. She watched from her bedroom window as they built a sandcastle together, a ridiculously elaborate construction that made her smile even as her heart gave a little pulsing ache of sorrow. She wanted to be down there on the beach with them. She wanted Angelos to want it, but she knew he didn't.

Finally, the next morning while Sofia was at her lessons, Talia confronted Angelos in his study.

His gaze sharpened and his mouth thinned as she stepped into his inner sanctum, trying not to let her fear show at his unwelcoming look.

'What is it?' he asked. 'I trust nothing is wrong with Sofia?'

'Actually,' Talia said as she closed the door, 'something is.'

Angelos straightened in his chair. 'What do you mean?'

'I spoke with her a few days ago, Angelos, and she said something that I think you need to know about.'

'Which is?'

'I asked her about going to school on Naxos…'

'You what?' His voice came out like a boom of thunder, and made her tremble nearly as much. 'You had no right—'

'I wanted to know if she'd ever considered going to school,' Talia replied stubbornly, locking her knees and lifting her chin. 'She had fun when we were on Naxos, and it seemed like a reasonable question to me…'

'You know why she doesn't want to go,' Angelos said in a low voice that thrummed with anger.

'I do now,' Talia returned. 'But do you?'

He glared at her, fury simmering in his eyes and a muscle flickering in his temple. Even angry he was gorgeous, and she still longed for him. 'What do you mean by that question?'

'Sofia told me *you* don't want her to go to school on Naxos.'

'I want her to be comfortable,' Angelos snapped. 'And protected. I've seen how she is when we're out in public. She hides her face—'

'From you.' Talia took a deep breath, knowing her next words would hurt, and perhaps even get her fired. 'I think she believes you are ashamed of her, Angelos. Of her scar.'

'What!' Angelos's voice came out in a crack like a gunshot, and he jerked back as if she'd been the one to fire the bullet. 'How can you even...? I have never been ashamed of it. *Never*. Why would she think such a thing?' He shook his head, his eyes snapping with fury and hurt. 'Why would you think it? Is that—is that the kind of man you believe I am?'

'*No,*' she said, her voice rising, ringing with sincerity, as tears pricked her eyes. 'No, Angelos, I don't. But when you are with her, you scowl and frown and seem very fierce—'

'If I scowl, it's because I hate the thought that she is self-conscious about it,' Angelos bit out. 'That she is ashamed. She has no reason to be. None. If anyone does, it is me.'

'What do you mean by that?' Talia asked. 'Why should you be ashamed, Angelos? What is it that keeps you—?'

'I failed her,' he said flatly. 'In the fire.'

'Because you couldn't protect her from getting hurt?' Talia surmised. 'But it wasn't your fault—'

'Actually, it was. But we will not discuss it.'

'Maybe you need to discuss it—'

'Did you not understand what I said to you before?' Angelos cut across her, his voice hard and flat. 'You are taking liberties, Miss Di Sione.'

'Don't "Miss Di Sione" me,' Talia snapped. She hated how Angelos hid behind cold formality. She *knew* he was hurting and afraid, but there was absolutely nothing she could do about it. She wouldn't humiliate herself again by insisting he really cared about her, or begging him to unburden himself to her. 'Just think about what I said.

And maybe ask Sofia if she would like to go to school on Naxos.'

Not trusting herself to say anything more or to keep herself from breaking down, Talia strode from the room, slamming the door with satisfying force behind her.

# CHAPTER THIRTEEN

ANGELOS REMAINED WHERE he stood, the echo of Talia's slamming the door reverberating through the room.

Was she right? Could Sofia possibly think that he was ashamed of her? In his letter he'd taken pains to tell her how proud he was of her, how beautiful he thought her. But maybe letters weren't enough. Maybe the way he acted when he was with her spoke louder than his cowardly written words. Because the truth was, looking at his daughter hurt *him*, because it reminded him of his own failures. But the possibility that it was hurting *her* was agony. Torture. He'd spent the last seven years trying to atone for his sins, working hard to keep Sofia feeling safe and protected. The idea that he'd failed utterly in his goal possessed the power to fell him. What if he, in his ineptitude and fear, had made things *worse*?

And Talia had had the courage to confront him about it, knowing he would be angry, that he would drive her away, just as he had done. She really was brave.

Sighing, Angelos sank into his chair. First he needed to talk to Sofia. He could deal with Talia later.

When Angelos came in that evening before bed to talk to Sofia, his expression serious, Talia's heart lifted even as her insides quailed with trepidation. She quietly excused

herself and when she returned an hour later, having heard
Angelos's slow, heavy tread down the stairs, Sofia had already fallen asleep.

Leaning close, Talia had been able to see the tracks of
tears on the girl's face and she'd bitten her lip, wondering
how the conversation between father and daughter had
gone. Angelos had made it abundantly clear that it was
not her place to ask.

She went back to her bedroom and watched the moon
rise above the sea, trying to enjoy the moment for what it
was. In two weeks she'd leave Kallos, leave Angelos and
Sofia behind for ever. But she hoped the things she'd ex-
perienced here, the lessons she'd learned, would equip her
to face her own future with more courage.

And what about Giovanni's book? Sighing, Talia sat on
her bed, wrapping her arms around her knees and resting her chin on top. She hated admitting her failure to her
grandfather, but what else could she do? At this point she
doubted Angelos even had the book. He'd certainly ex-
pressed no interest in poetry.

But then she hadn't tried very hard at all. The least her
grandfather deserved was for her to make a proper attempt.
And she didn't really have anything left to lose when it
came to her relationship, or lack of it, with Angelos.

Before she left, Talia promised herself, she'd ask him
straight out. At least then she could go back to Giovanni
with a clear conscience and a conviction that she'd done
the best she could.

She only wished she felt that way about her relationship with Angelos and Sofia. What if she'd made things
worse, by telling Angelos her fears about Sofia's feelings? What if too much honesty had damaged their fragile
father-daughter relationship?

Restless now, she rose from the bed and went downstairs, intending to take a walk on the beach to clear her head. The light filtering under Angelos's study door made her pause on the bottom stair, wondering if she dared go in and ask him how his conversation with Sofia had gone.

The thought of facing his stony-faced fury a second time made her falter, and after another second's hesitation she continued on to the front door. She'd just put a hand on the latch when she heard a sound coming from Angelos's study—something between a moan and a sob—and then the shattering of glass.

Her breath catching in her throat, her heart beating hard, Talia turned back to his study. She could not ignore those sounds of grief and despair, yet she also cringed at the thought of Angelos's rage. Hesitantly she tapped on the door and when there was no answer, she turned the handle and pushed the door open with her fingertips.

Angelos sat sprawled in a chair by the fireplace, shattered glass sprinkling the hearth and the strong anise smell of ouzo permeating the air.

'Angelos…'

He glanced up at her, his hair rumpled, the buttons of his shirt half undone, his gaze bleary. 'I'm not drunk, if that's what you're afraid of,' he said. 'I haven't had so much as a sip.'

'I suppose that accounts for the smell and the broken glass,' Talia said as she closed the door.

Angelos glanced indifferently at the shards of glass surrounding him. 'I suppose it does.'

'No point in cutting yourself,' Talia said, and bent to pick up the larger pieces. She swept them into her hand and then looked around for the bin.

'Beneath the desk.' Angelos's eyes were closed, his face a ravaged mask of pain. 'Thank you.'

She got rid of the glass and then sat gingerly in the chair opposite him. 'Do you want to talk about it?'

'No.'

'That's not actually a surprise.'

He cracked open an eye and stared at her. 'You can joke?'

'I don't know what to do,' Talia admitted. 'Let me help you, Angelos. I can tell you're hurting.'

He closed his eyes again. 'You have no idea.'

'I know I don't. So tell me.' He just shook his head and she expelled an impatient breath. 'You are the most stubborn, mule-headed man I've ever met!'

He smiled faintly at that, the barest quirk of his lips, but at least it was a reaction. 'I must be.'

'It's as if you *want* to be miserable—'

He opened an eye, arched an eyebrow. 'A glutton for punishment?'

'It appears we both are,' Talia answered, a flush touching her cheeks as she remembered how she'd practically begged for Angelos to care about her. The memory was enough to make her admit defeat. 'Fine. You know what, Angelos? You can stew here for as long as you like. Drown in ouzo if you want to.' She took a trembling breath. 'You gave me the courage to face my fears but it seems I am not able to give you the same. So I give up.' She turned towards the door, blinking back tears, hating how much this man affected her. How much she wanted to help him and couldn't.

'Talia.' Her name was a whisper as she put her hand on the doorknob. 'Don't go.'

Slowly Talia turned around. 'Do you mean that?'

His eyes were closed, his expression bleak. The word, when it came, was barely audible. 'Yes.'

Silently she returned to her chair, and then sat down and waited, her hands clenched in her lap, her heart beating hard.

Angelos let out a long, low breath and opened his eyes. 'I spoke to Sofia tonight, as you know. She told me…she told me the same thing you had told me. That she thought I was ashamed of her. That I kept her on this island to hide her from people, because I didn't want anyone to see her scar.' He scrubbed his face with his hands. 'If I'd known that she would think that…the damage I would cause, on top of everything else…' He shook his head. 'I am the one who is ashamed. Of so much.'

'What are you ashamed of?' Talia asked softly.

She didn't think Angelos was going to answer. He remained silent for a long time, his hands still covering his face, and then he slowly dropped them and stared at her. Talia nearly gasped at the utter bleakness she saw there.

'Because,' Angelos said heavily, 'it was my fault that there was a fire.' Talia knew instinctively there was more, and so she remained silent, waiting and alert. After an endless moment Angelos continued. 'I was working downstairs. It had been a hard week, sleepless nights… Sofia was teething.' He let out a sound that he choked off as soon as it came out of him, pressing the back of his hand to his mouth. 'She was such a sweet baby. So good-natured. Xanthe and I were so blessed. I'd never thought to have a wife, a family. Me, a gutter rat from the docks.' He shook his head, lost in memory, awash in grief.

'What happened, Angelos?' Talia asked quietly. 'That night?'

'Xanthe was upstairs with Sofia. She was rocking her in the nursery. We lived in Athens at the time, a town house in Kolonaki. An old building, with leaky pipes and faulty wires…'

'It was an electrical fire?' Talia guessed, and Angelos nodded, his face twisted in regret.

'I always meant to have the building inspected. I knew it was old—I picked it up for a song...'

'You can't blame yourself for that,' Talia protested. 'An electrical fire could happen to anyone, anywhere...'

'It wasn't just that.' He drove his fingers through his hair, his head bowed. 'I'd been drinking. A couple of glasses of ouzo, while I worked on reports. But I was tired and it must have affected me more than I'd thought because I was so slow.' He dropped his hands and looked at her openly then, his pain naked, his face screwed up in anguish. 'Talia, I was too *slow*.'

'Oh, Angelos.' His name caught in her throat and she blinked back tears as she realised the depth of the agony he'd endured then, and in the seven years since. Unthinkingly she dropped to her knees in front of him and took his hands in hers. 'Tell me,' she whispered.

'It started in the nursery.' He bowed his head, his hands clenched in hers. 'The door was shut, and Xanthe had fallen asleep in the rocker with Sofia. By the time the alarm went off and I smelled the smoke, the fire was already raging. Xanthe was screaming, *screaming*...she couldn't get the door open. The heat had swollen it shut. I tried to kick it down, I shoved my whole body against it over and over again, but I couldn't. And the fire brigade was taking so *long*...' His hands tightened on hers, hard enough to make Talia wince, but nothing would make her let go of Angelos now. 'Xanthe told me to leave. She knew...she knew she couldn't get out, but she wanted to save Sofia. She told me to go downstairs and she would throw her to me.'

'Oh, Angelos...'

'I refused. I refused, Talia, because I still wanted to save my wife. By the time I finally realised I couldn't and ran downstairs, Sofia had already been burned. If I'd only listened…if I'd have acted faster…' He shook his head. 'Xanthe threw her down to me, and as I held our daughter, the flames engulfed her.' A tear splashed onto her hand and wordlessly Talia put her arms around Angelos. He pressed his head against her chest, seeking comfort.

'The fire brigade came then,' he continued in a choked voice. 'Too late. Too damned late. And Sofia's face was badly burned, and parts of her body…she was so *little*. She spent six months in hospital, having to have skin grafts and surgeries. It was hell for both of us. She was in terrible pain and she missed her mother. She cried constantly— she didn't want me, not even to hold her. She didn't understand any of what had happened and I was so useless…' He let out a choked sob and shook his head. 'So useless, in so many ways.'

'Oh, Angelos,' Talia whispered as she stroked his hair. 'How terrible for both of you. I'm so, so sorry.'

Neither of them spoke for a long moment and then finally Angelos eased away, his head still lowered. 'It was easier to keep my distance from her afterwards. I bought Kallos and employed a nanny who could give her the care I never could. I thought I was doing the right thing, the best thing, for Sofia. But maybe I was just being selfish, keeping my distance because I couldn't bear to be reminded of my own failings.' He shook his head. 'And I just made things worse.'

'But you can make them better now,' Talia insisted. 'Sofia is only nine, and she needs you. She loves you. Make things better now, and love her back.'

'I do love her—'

'Spend time with her. Live on Kallos, or bring her to Athens with you. Show her and the world that you're not ashamed of her.'

Angelos lifted his head and gazed at her, his brown

eyes damp, his thick, dark lashes spiky. 'How did a young woman like you become so wise?'

Talia let out a self-conscious laugh. 'Am I really so wise? I've hidden away for the last seven years rather than face reality or try to conquer my anxiety. It's easy to speak to someone else's situation.'

'But you conquered your anxiety in coming here.'

'Yes.' Her throat dried at the intent look in Angelos's eyes, the realisation of how close his face was to hers. 'And for that I am truly thankful,' she managed to continue, 'to you.'

'You have nothing to thank me for.'

'I do—'

'I was a right bastard to you when you arrived.'

'Well, maybe,' she allowed with a little laugh. 'But I've seen how kind you are.' She tried for a playful smile. 'Your secret is out, Angelos.'

'Is it?' he asked, his voice low and aching, and Talia's heart gave a hopeful thump, like the tail wagging on a dog.

'I think so…' she murmured, and her mouth was so dry she touched her tongue to her lips, eliciting a groan from Angelos.

'Talia…' He wrapped one hand around the back of her neck, his fingers warm and strong and sure. 'Talia, you drive me crazy…'

'Do I?' she whispered, and then he was pulling her towards him and his lips were on hers, seeking and finding her as she'd wanted for so long, since the last time he'd kissed her.

Talia reached up and tangled her hands in his hair, anchoring his mouth more firmly to hers. She couldn't get enough of him, of the taste and feel and sheer beauty of him as he slid his hands from her neck to her shoulders, pulling her from her kneeling position to sprawl on his lap as his mouth plundered hers.

Her heart raced as sensations exploded in her like fireworks, each one more intense than the last. Angelos's hand sliding under her shirt, his palm flat on her belly, and then moving upwards, cupping the warm fullness of her breast, his thumb brushing its aching peak…

How did anyone survive this? she wondered hazily as she kissed him back with untutored enthusiasm and passion. How did anyone feel this way and live?

Then Angelos tore his mouth from hers, his breath coming out in a gasp. 'We shouldn't…'

'We should,' Talia insisted. She would not be put off a second time. 'Angelos, I—' *I love you* bubbled on her lips but she swallowed the words down. He didn't want to hear that. Not yet, and probably not ever. 'I want you,' she said instead, and his expression darkened, his pupils dilating.

'I want you too. Very much so.'

'Then why not?'

'It will complicate things—'

She glanced down at her rucked-up shirt, her legs sprawled across his lap, the hard and intriguing bulge of his arousal against her calf. 'Things are already pretty complicated.'

Angelos let out a groan and leaned his head back against the chair. 'Talia, you're going to kill me.'

'Then surely it will be a pleasant death?' Some inner vixen emboldened her to press her palms against his chest, stroking the hard planes of muscles, teasing his nipples. She ached to touch him, and the evidence of his response as he groaned again and his body stirred was utterly thrilling. She leaned forward, her hair brushing his cheek, and pressed a kiss to his lips. 'Please, Angelos,' she whispered, 'don't make me beg.'

He caught her face in his hands and forced her to meet his fierce gaze. 'If you're sure?'

'Of course I'm sure.'

Angelos stared at her for a long, hard moment and then he nodded. 'All right, then. Come with me,' he said, and in one fluid movement he caught her up in his arms and strode from the study, up the stairs and to his bedroom.

# CHAPTER FOURTEEN

ANTICIPATION RACED THROUGH Talia as she hooked her arms around Angelos's neck and held on. He entered his bedroom, kicking the door closed behind him, before he deposited Talia on the huge bed, its dark silken sheets slippery beneath her.

She stared up at him, her eyes wide as he began to unbutton his shirt. She'd seen his bare chest before when they'd gone swimming but she'd never seen him like this— eyes dark, liquid and burning with intensity, his long, elegant fingers slipping his buttons out of their holes, his gaze never leaving hers.

She let out her breath in a shaky rush and wondered if she should tell him how untouched she was. But surely he knew? Since she'd confessed to living like a hermit for seven years?

'You're not having second thoughts?' Angelos asked in a low voice.

'No, of course not.' Her whole body throbbed and ached with the need to feel him again. Touch him again.

'I don't have any birth control,' he told her, his hands stilling on his shirt as his gaze widened in realisation. 'I've never…' Talia gaped in astonishment as a light blush touched his cheekbones. 'I haven't needed any here.'

'I'm on the pill,' Talia assured him. She'd been on it

since she was sixteen, to regulate her heavy periods. 'And as for…other stuff, I'm not…that is, I'm…' She was trying to tell him she was a virgin, but Angelos cut her off with a nod.

'So am I.' Somehow she didn't think he was talking about virginity. 'Clear,' he clarified, and she realised she must have been looking blank.

'Oh. Right. Well, then…' The moment for telling Angelos she was a virgin had passed. Talia didn't want to ruin the mood, and he seemed like the kind of man who might scruple at taking a woman's virginity.

'It's all good,' he said, his smile turning wolfish as he finished unbuttoning his shirt and shrugged the crisp white cotton from his glorious shoulders. Talia was glad not to have to explain, especially since she seemed to have lost the ability to speak or even to think. Angelos, with his hair rumpled, his eyes burning and his chest bare, was an utterly magnificent sight.

She watched, her mouth dry and her heart pounding, as his hands went to his belt buckle, and then stopped.

'Don't…' she breathed, and he frowned.

'Don't what?'

'Don't stop,' she clarified on a groan and, amazed at her own audacity, she reached for him, her fingers sliding around his belt buckle so she could tug him towards her.

He put one arm out to brace his fall, landing beside her on the bed, his body lean and hard, hot and bare. Gently Talia skimmed her fingers along his chest, her fingers brushing the crisp dark hair, teasing, questing.

'I've been wanting to do this for a while,' she admitted on a laugh, and then because she couldn't keep herself from it, she pressed a kiss to his chest. Angelos groaned and rolled onto his back, taking her with him.

'You are so very sweet.'

'I'm… I'm not sure I'm very good at this,' she confessed, which was as close as she was willing to come to admitting she was completely inexperienced.

'Trust me, you are very good at this,' Angelos said. He slid his hands under her T-shirt, his palms exquisitely rough against the smooth skin of her back. With one swift tug he had the shirt up and over her head and she struggled to pull it off, laughing breathlessly until her naked breasts came into contact with his chest and then she gasped in the sheer pleasure of the sensation.

'*Oh*…that feels good.'

Angelos grinned up at her as he started to tug off her shorts. 'We're just beginning.'

Another tug and her shorts were gone, and she lay before him completely naked, utterly exposed, and yet she felt no nervousness or vulnerability. She basked in his appreciative stare, the way his pupils flared as his gaze roved over her.

He reached out and cupped her breast, his thumb moving slowly over the peak. Talia arched up helplessly to meet his hand.

'You are so beautiful,' Angelos rasped, his eyes dark with desire.

'*You're* beautiful,' she answered on a gasp, and he laughed softly before he put his mouth to her breast and Talia gasped again, her hands fisting in his hair, as pleasure rippled through her in exquisite shocks. '*Oh…*' She sucked in a hard breath as he moved his mouth to her other breast. 'Oh, I didn't *know…*'

He lifted his head to glance at her, lazily amused. 'Didn't know what?'

'That you could feel…' She trailed off, overcome, because Angelos was giving her so much, showing her so much. *If she hadn't come to Greece…if she hadn't been able to feel this way, to know you could feel this way…*

It didn't matter that it would end in a few weeks or even that night, Talia told herself fiercely. It didn't matter if she left Greece heartbroken and alone. She had this, and it would be enough. She would never regret it.

'Talia…' Angelos propped himself up one elbow as he looked down at her, his smile soft, his expression unbearably tender. 'Talia, are you all right?'

She realised how close she was to weeping, not with sorrow, but with sheer emotion. With joy. 'I'm fine,' she assured him, and kissed him hard, wrapping her arms around him, pressing her naked body to his. 'I'm completely and utterly wonderful.'

Angelos caught her up in the kiss, his tongue tangling with hers as his arms came around her, clasping her to him.

He flipped her onto her back, making her let out a sudden laugh of surprise, and then slowly he slid his hand down her body, savouring each dip and curve before he pressed his palm to the juncture of her thighs.

Talia let out a little yelp of shock and Angelos glanced at her, one eyebrow quirked in question.

'That feels…'

'Good?' he finished as his fingers touched her more intimately than she'd ever imagined.

'Yes,' she gasped as her hips arched instinctively. 'Yes…'

She felt her body convulse as pleasure ripped through her in deepening waves, so an instinct she hadn't even known she'd possessed took over, driving her forward. She grabbed Angelos's hand with both of her own, and he gave a low laugh as his fingers worked their deft magic.

'I'm not going anywhere,' he assured her.

'You'd better not,' she breathed, and then pleasure gripped her like a vice before releasing her in a breathless daze. 'Oh…'

In one fluid movement Angelos rolled over her before he slid smoothly inside, only to stop before he'd barely begun, shock turning his body rigid. 'Talia…'

She blinked, surprised and a little alarmed at how…*full* it felt. 'I'm okay,' she said.

Angelos's jaw was clenched as he struggled to keep himself still inside her body. 'But—'

'I'm okay,' she insisted, and she angled her hips upwards to take him more fully into her body. It hurt; not a sudden, sharp pain, but more of a deep ache of adjustment.

Angelos's face was etched with lines of restraint and regret. 'I didn't…'

'No, don't, please.' She pressed her fingers against her lips. 'This is what I wanted.' She shifted beneath him, felt her body expand to accommodate him. 'This is good.'

'Tell me if—'

'It doesn't hurt, I promise.'

Angelos started to move, a groan escaping him as he braced himself on his forearms and after a few seconds Talia sought to match each smooth stroke. And with each stroke she felt the embers of pleasure rekindle, and then her body found a rhythm of its own. She clutched at his shoulders, meeting each thrust, gasping as it stoked the fire inside her higher and higher, until finally it exploded in a rush of sensation that left her boneless and trembling, tears leaking from beneath her closed lids.

'Talia,' Angelos said brokenly as he kissed the tears away from her cheeks. 'Please don't cry.'

'It's only because I'm so happy.' She opened her eyes, giving him a watery smile. She still felt as if she could burst into tears, but not in a bad way. 'That was…amazing. Overwhelming. I didn't know…'

'Why didn't you tell me you didn't know?' Angelos asked. He'd rolled over onto his side, his skin glistening with a faint sheen of sweat, his eyes dark and fierce. 'How much you didn't know?'

'I was afraid you wouldn't want to go through with it,' Talia confessed.

'You should have told me,' Angelos insisted as he brushed away a strand of hair from her cheek, tucking it gently behind her ear. 'I would have done things differently.'

'I didn't want things done differently. And actually, I thought you might already guess… I told you how limited my life was.'

'Yes, but…' Angelos shrugged. 'You're a beautiful young woman. I thought you must have still had opportunities.'

Talia shook her head ruefully. 'I dated a boy when I was seventeen, and we kissed a couple of times. That's all.'

Angelos's eyebrows rose almost comically. 'That's all? But then you were completely untouched.'

'I wasn't all that interested in boys to be honest,' Talia told him. 'I wanted adventure of a different kind. Seeing the world, painting pictures…that was what interested me.'

'Which makes it all the more tragic that you hid yourself away for so long.'

'I'm not going to hide away any more,' Talia promised. 'No matter what happens. I want to live life properly now.' Angelos frowned and she hastened to add, 'I'm not expecting… I know we haven't made any…' A flush rose to her skin and since she was naked Angelos could see how she blushed everywhere. She let out a groan of embarrassment as she closed her eyes.

'Haven't made any what, Talia?' Angelos asked, and she couldn't tell if he was amused or annoyed.

'Commitments. I just wanted to assure you I didn't expect any kind of…' Again words failed her. 'You know.'

'I'm not sure I do know,' Angelos answered. He cupped her cheek, his thumb resting on her lips, and Talia opened her eyes. 'You know, you're the first woman I've been with since my wife.'

'What?' Talia stared at him in shock. 'I know you said you hadn't recently, but it's been seven years…'

'Trust me, I know. A very long seven years, at least in that regard.'

'Why haven't you…? I mean, there must have been women in Athens.' Her mouth curved in a playful smile that he traced with the pad of his thumb. 'And what about all those nannies who crawled into your bed? Maria told me about them.'

Angelos gave a mock shudder. 'I did not want any of them. They were brazen, grasping. But the truth is…' He let out a sigh. 'I had no desire for a woman, or for any of life's pleasures. I felt numb…frozen even, after all the fire and then its aftermath. Survival was all I could manage. And like you, I hid away from life.' He grimaced. 'And now I have realised that Sofia paid the price.'

'And, like me, you won't hide away any more,' Talia said softly. 'Will you?'

'No. For Sofia's sake I will allow her to go to school on Naxos, and come to Athens with me on business trips. I decided that tonight. I'm not ashamed of my daughter, Talia.'

'I know you're not.' Fresh tears shimmered on her lashes and she blinked them away. 'You're a good man, Angelos, even if you haven't believed you are. I know you did everything you could the night of the fire, even if you refused to believe it. You couldn't have saved them both. You *couldn't* have.'

Angelos's face contorted for a second and then he threw his arm over his face as he took a few deep breaths. 'I know you believe that…' he began, and Talia pulled at his arm, needing to look at him, to have him see her and how serious she was.

'*You* need to believe it,' she said. 'For Sofia's sake as well as your own.'

'I'm not sure I can.'

She pressed her palm on his chest, felt the steady thud of his heart underneath. 'In time, then,' she said softly. 'I know it isn't easy. One boat ride doesn't cure my claustrophobia, and living life outside the walls of my grandfather's estate isn't going to be easy. But with time, all things are possible.'

'You believe that?'

'I need to. And so do you.'

He let out a sigh and then gathered her into his arms, resting his chin on top of her head. 'Thank you,' he whispered. 'For giving me a second chance at life.'

'You deserve one.' They lay there quietly for a moment, their arms around each other, and Talia wondered if she would ever possess the courage to say all the things in her heart. That she loved him. That she didn't want this to be some kind of fling. That she was already dreaming of for ever with this man, even though she knew it was crazy and unrealistic and maybe even impossible.

*But what if it wasn't?*

What if they could have a love that healed their old hurts and brought them both a second chance at life, made them into the family Sofia needed, that they needed? *What if?*

In that moment, with Angelos's arms around her so securely, it all seemed possible, like a promise shimmering on the horizon, almost able to be grasped if she just dared to reach for it. If they both did.

Angelos stroked her hair and she snuggled against him, contentment vibrating through her bones, sleep beginning to settle over her.

Her eyes were starting to drift closed when her gaze settled on the book lying on the bedside table. A slender, leather-bound tome with hand-tooled engraving. Giovanni's book.

Her gaze snapped open and every nerve twanged with realisation as she struggled out of Angelos's embrace.

'Talia…' His voice was fuzzy with sleep. 'What…'

'The book,' she said, the words spilling from her. 'You really do have the book.'

She felt Angelos's body stiffen in surprise and he propped himself up one arm. 'Book? What book?'

'This…' Reverently Talia reached for the book of poetry. The leather was butter-soft and worn. She flipped the book open and let out a gasp of both surprise and satisfaction at the sight of the inscription, which she read aloud: '"Dearest Lucia, For ever in my heart, always. B.A."' She smiled, feeling emotional all over again. 'Just like he told me.'

Belatedly Talia registered the tension emanating from Angelos's body. He withdrew from her, sitting up, his arms folded across his chest. 'Just like *who* told you, Talia? And how the *hell* do you know about my wife's book?'

# CHAPTER FIFTEEN

ANGELOS WATCHED AS Talia slowly closed the book and turned to him, her smile sliding off her face, her eyes shadowing, her shoulders starting to hunch. Guilt. That was what was written on her face, all over her body, in bold, stark letters. *Guilt.*

'Well?' he bit out. 'Do you have an answer?' He didn't even know what to think, how to process what she had said. How could Talia possibly know about Xanthe's precious book? And what on earth had she meant, he really did have it? Suspicions formed on the horizon of his mind, a boiling black cloud of fear and anger that was moving closer, drowning out all rational thought. 'Why can't you explain it to me?'

'I can,' she said. Her voice sounded small and she was clutching the book to her chest.

'Put down the book,' Angelos barked out, driven by a deep and overwhelming emotion he couldn't name; he only felt himself trapped in its clutches. 'Don't you dare touch it.'

Talia's gaze widened and carefully she returned the book to his bedside table. 'I'm sorry.'

'So am I.' Angelos rolled out of bed, swearing under his breath as he reached for his clothes.

'Angelos, please. Don't…'

'Don't what? Ask questions? Demand answers? Why do I feel like there is something you are not telling me? Something big?'

'There is,' she admitted, and her words were like a hammer blow to his fragile, taped-together heart. Everything inside him shattered. She leaned forward, kneading the sheet between her fingers, her golden-brown hair falling over her freckled shoulders, making him desire her even now, a realisation that sent disgust following hard after. 'But, Angelos, please,' she said. 'It doesn't *have* to be big.'

'Why don't you let me be the judge of that,' he snapped, and yanked on his trousers.

'Please,' she whispered. 'If you could just see…'

'See what? That you lied to me?' He grabbed his shirt and thrust his arms through the sleeves. 'Because that's what you did, isn't it?' He pointed to the book lying on the bedside table, the book his wife had cherished. 'How did you know about that book?'

Talia swallowed hard, the muscles jerking in her slender throat. 'My grandfather once owned it. It was a treasured possession of his.'

'Another lie,' Angelos dismissed. 'That book has been in my wife's family for generations.' She paled at that and he gave a hard, derisive laugh. 'So what is it really, Talia? Are you after the book because it's valuable?'

She drew back in shock. 'Valuable? You think I'm after your *money*?'

'The book has been valued at fifty thousand pounds. It's an extremely rare edition.'

'I don't want or need your money,' she spat. 'My grandfather is Giovanni Di Sione, of Di Sione Shipping—'

'Impressive,' Angelos cut across her, his voice a furious drawl. 'Other things you didn't feel you needed to tell me.'

'You didn't ask,' Talia protested. 'I mentioned my grandfather's estate…'

Of course she had. And looking back, Angelos realised he'd known she was from money. The clues she'd dropped about the estate, her studio, the travelling she'd done. Of course she was rich.

'It doesn't matter,' he stated flatly. 'I don't care about your grandfather or his estate.'

'But it's because of my grandfather that I was looking for that book,' Talia said quietly. She was clutching handfuls of sheet in her fists, her knuckles as blazing white against the dark silk. 'It did belong to him, Angelos, a long time ago. It was very precious to him.'

'The book belonged to my wife's grandmother,' Angelos told her. 'She was a lady's maid for a duchess on Isola d'Oro. The duchess gave it to her as a parting gift.'

Talia frowned, shaking her head slowly. 'I don't understand. My grandfather is from Italy. But I know it was his. He told me about the inscription on the front page.'

'"Dearest Lucia, For ever in my heart, always. B.A."' Angelos turned away abruptly, not wanting Talia to see the expression on his face. Not wanting to feel the pain that rose up in him. He and Xanthe had said the same thing to each other. *For ever in our hearts, always.* 'My wife loved that book,' he said tonelessly. 'It was her prized possession. She kept it on her bedside table. It was the only thing saved from the fire, and that only because I'd had it in the safe in my office. I'd just had it valued for insurance. I was going to return it to Xanthe that night.' Talia made a small, abject sound, and feeling cold and emotionless now, Angelos turned around. 'And you want to what? Buy it off me?'

'My grandfather asked me to find it for him,' Talia

said in a small voice. 'I didn't realise how important it was to you…'

'How did you trace it to me?' Angelos asked. 'Out of interest?'

'I found a website dealing in finding rare books. Someone from Mena Consultancy had put a query forth about other books by the same poet.'

'Ah, yes.' His gut soured as he remembered. 'I tried to find a second book for my wife's birthday, years ago.' He shook his head. 'And you came all the way here for that.'

'Yes…'

'That's why you were in my office in the first place,' he surmised. Realisation after realisation thudded sickly through him. 'Not to apply for the nanny position as I'd assumed.'

'No, but—'

'And you didn't see fit to tell me? You could have cleared up my misunderstanding in minutes. In *seconds*.'

'I know, but it was difficult. I was tired and overwhelmed by travelling all that way, and then when I realised I could help Sofia…'

'And snoop around for the book as well, no doubt.'

Talia swallowed, a gulping motion. 'Not snoop, but yes, I thought I'd be able to look…'

'That's why you asked me about poetry on the boat, isn't it?' Angelos said with a disgusted shake of his head. 'I thought it an odd question, but I believed you were just trying to get to know me.' The exposure that admission caused, the realisation that he'd *wanted* her to get to know him, had him turning away.

'I *was* trying to get to know you,' Talia whispered. 'I wanted—'

'Enough.' Angelos slashed his hand through the air. '*Enough.* I can't bear to hear any more of your pathetic excuses. Leave me.' He turned around, watched as tears filled her eyes and her fingers trembled on the sheet.

'Angelos, please. I know I should have said something earlier, but I was starting to care about Sofia, about you, and it seemed so difficult to admit—'

'*Go,*' Angelos roared, and he turned around, unable to face her. He heard her rise from the bed and scramble for her clothes, and then the soft, quick tread of her feet and the click of the door closing.

He let out a shuddering sigh and raked his hands through his hair, grief and guilt and deep, deep regret coursing through him in an unbearable torrent. He'd *trusted* her. He'd told her more than he'd told anyone, even Xanthe. Xanthe hadn't wanted to know about his deprived childhood, the hard lessons he'd learned. Yet Talia had seemed interested, sympathetic, kind. All of it an act to get what she wanted.

A remote part of him insisted he was being unfair, judging Talia so harshly. He could understand why she'd be reluctant to speak up, and yet…

She'd lied. And she would be leaving anyway. The night they'd shared together, and so much more than a single, simple night, had been a mistake. That much Angelos knew with leaden certainty.

Talia crept into her bed and lay there shivering despite the sultry night air. She'd ruined everything by not coming clean to Angelos. Why hadn't she told him about her grandfather and the wretched book earlier? The answer was depressingly obvious. Because she'd been afraid. Afraid of Angelos's anger, of losing what they had together. And so she'd waited, and now she'd lost so much more.

But perhaps she'd never had it to begin with. She

thought of the grief and pain she'd seen so nakedly on Angelos's face. He'd loved his wife. Perhaps he still loved her. Perhaps she and Angelos had never had even a whisper of a chance of a future together.

Eventually Talia drifted into a restless doze, only to wake as dawn's pale grey light filtered through the shutters. She listened to the birdsong and the gentle shooshing of the waves on the beach and knew she had only one choice. She'd have to leave. Better to leave than be fired, which Angelos surely intended to do, and she couldn't endure another week of being with Angelos and having him hate her. Knowing she'd wrecked any hope of a future together.

Sofia's new nanny would arrive in a matter of days, and Talia knew she would be leaving the girl in good hands. Perhaps Angelos could have a few days alone with his daughter, or Maria could manage. She wouldn't be leaving anyone in the lurch if she went now, a thought that still managed to hurt her. She wasn't needed, not really.

With a leaden heart she showered and dressed and then packed her few possessions. The lovely silk Angelos had bought on Naxos she left, still in its paper wrappings. Perhaps he could have a dress made for Sofia.

Downstairs she went directly to Angelos's study and knocked on the door. His terse, 'Enter,' had her insides trembling but she lifted her chin, opened the door and walked in.

'Yes?' Angelos's cold stare was unwelcoming, his lips compressed into a hard line. It seemed incredible to Talia that last night he'd held her in his arms, she'd drawn him into her body. She'd been happier than she'd ever been before.

She blinked the images away and forced herself to

speak. 'I thought it best if I leave. Your new nanny is coming soon anyway, and I'm sure Maria can manage on her own for a little while, or perhaps you and Sofia can spend some more time together. But I think I'll just be… in the way.'

Angelos didn't answer and Talia forced herself not to look away from the cold, assessing stare that reminded her so painfully of the man she'd first met, back in Athens.

'Very well,' he finally answered tonelessly. 'I will arrange for the helicopter to pick you up this afternoon.'

'Thank you,' she whispered.

'You will manage?' Angelos asked. 'In the helicopter?'

'Yes, I think so.' Tears sprang to her eyes at the realisation that even now Angelos was concerned for her. It almost made her want to stay, to *try*… 'Angelos…' she began, and he looked up from his laptop screen.

'There is nothing more to say.' He cut her off in a clipped voice. 'You may say your goodbyes to Sofia.'

Swallowing hard she nodded and turned from the room.

Her farewell to Sofia was awful, worse than anything Talia could have imagined.

'But you *stay*,' Sofia exclaimed as tears started in her eyes. 'Stay. *Parakalo.*' Not having the English to say more, the little girl simply stared at Talia, imploring her with her eyes just as she had back in Athens. This time Talia had to refuse.

'I can write,' she said, miming the action. 'Emails and letters.' Although she wondered if Angelos would allow it. 'Take care, Sofia. *S'agapo.*'

'I love you too,' Sofia answered in English, and then broke down into noisy tears.

Two hours later Talia walked alone from the villa, her suitcase in hand, to the waiting helicopter. She felt emotionless and empty now, and she clambered up into the helicopter without so much as a twinge of fear.

Heartbreak trumped claustrophobia perhaps, she acknowledged as she sat down and buckled herself in. The helicopter lifted off, and no one came to a window or door to say goodbye. Talia watched the island of Kallos grow smaller and smaller and finally disappear over the endless blue horizon.

Twenty-four hours later she was back on her grandfather's estate, the muggy warmth of a mid-August afternoon oppressive after Kallos's dry heat and sea breezes.

The house was quiet as she entered, the rooms seeming to echo with silence all around her. She let out a long sigh, feeling both emotional and physical exhaustion in every muscle and sinew.

'Miss Talia!' Alma, her grandfather's housekeeper, came bustling towards her. 'You're back. You sent no word.'

'I'm sorry. I didn't have time.'

'It's all right, of course,' Alma assured her. 'Your grandfather will be so pleased to have you back home.'

'How is he?' Talia asked. She'd been in regular email contact with Giovanni, but she knew he would never mention any health concerns to her, especially when she was so far away.

'Tired,' Alma said with a small, sad smile. 'But in good spirits. He's upstairs in his usual room. He's just woken up, if you'd like to see him. Dante and Willow are here as well.'

Talia knew she'd have to tell Giovanni that she had been unsuccessful in retrieving his book, and she decided it would be better to get it over with sooner rather than later, and so with a nod she headed upstairs.

Giovanni was in a small sitting room that adjoined his bedroom, a blanket over his legs despite the heat, frowning as he clicked the remote control of the TV.

He glanced over as she opened the door, his wrinkled face breaking into a huge smile as he caught sight of her. 'Talia, *cara*! You have returned.' He held out his arms and Talia went to him, kissing his withered cheek and embracing him lightly before she sat down across from his chair. 'You do not look happy, *cara*,' Giovanni said. 'What has happened?'

'I wasn't able to get your book, Nonno. I'm sorry.'

Giovanni didn't answer for a moment; he simply stared at her, his gaze almost as assessing as Angelos's had been. 'But you tried, yes?' he finally said, and she nodded.

'Yes. And I did find it. But the book is very special to its current owner. It belonged to his late wife.'

'Did it?' Giovanni nodded slowly and leaned back in his chair.

'Apparently her grandmother was a lady's maid to a duchess on some island. The duchess gave it to her as a parting gift.'

'Ah. I see.' Giovanni closed his eyes briefly, and Talia wondered what he wasn't saying. 'I'm sorry,' she said again.

'It is no matter, Talia. But I don't think this unhappiness I see in you comes simply from not being successful in the task I set you.' He opened his eyes and gazed at her with kind shrewdness. 'Does it?'

'No,' she confessed, and couldn't manage any more. Her throat had gone tight and she blinked rapidly.

'Ah, Talia. I wanted you to see more of the world, to kindle the spark I know still lives in you for adventure, for life. But I fear I quenched it instead.'

'You didn't, Nonno,' Talia assured him. 'It's only…

living is hard sometimes. Feeling everything so much. You know?'

'Yes.' He smiled at her sadly and then reached out to clasp her hand. 'I know.'

Days passed by and Talia didn't leave the estate. She walked its manicured grounds, reacquainting herself with its beauty even as she yearned for the rocky hills and white sand beaches of Kallos. She missed Angelos and Sofia with an intensity that was like a physical pain; it kept her from eating and sleeping, leaving her hollow-eyed and gaunt.

Alma scolded her and tried to ply her with food and Talia attempted a few meals to appease the concerned housekeeper, but she couldn't stave off the sorrow that swamped her soul.

Finally, at the end of August, Giovanni confronted her. It had been two long weeks since she'd left Kallos, and she'd done no more than drag herself through each day.

'Cara, I can tell you are hurting,' Giovanni said without preamble. 'And I recognise the hurt it is. You are heartbroken.'

Talia managed a wobbly smile at her grandfather's astuteness. 'Maybe. I've never known what that feels like before.'

'I did not send you away to break your heart,' Giovanni said sternly. 'I sent you away to discover it again. This will not do, Talia. You must live—and love—once more.'

Talia nodded wearily. 'I want to, Nonno, but...'

'But nothing. I have arranged for a local gallery to showcase your work in two weeks' time.'

Talia's mouth dropped open. 'What...'

'I know you have resisted such public appearances before, but you know very well that many galleries have clamoured for your work. Every year they ask. It is time for you to appease them, Talia. It is time for you to show yourself to the world.'

# CHAPTER SIXTEEN

'You're not wearing that, surely?'

'What?' Talia looked down at her plain mint-green shift. It was the morning of her exhibition; and she'd taken care with her appearance, or at least she'd thought she had. 'This is one of my best dresses,' she told Willow, the fiancée of her brother Dante. They'd arrived a few days ago, as had many of her siblings, for her gallery exhibition today, but beyond a few conversations she hadn't seen much of either Willow or Dante, secluded as they were on one of the estate's private cottages.

Nerves fluttered in her stomach as she thought about what she was going to do this afternoon. Show her artwork to the world, rather than keep to private portraits. Circulate among the crowds, conquer her anxiety and claustrophobia. Hopefully.

Since her grandfather's pep talk Talia had realised she wanted to move on, even though it was hard, and maybe even impossible. She'd selected the paintings she was proudest of for the exhibition, excitement and anxiety coursing through her at the thought of showing them to the world. But the artwork she was most proud of was one that wouldn't be on display; it was a sketch of Angelos and Sofia that she had, after much deliberation, sent to him on Kallos.

It had been amazingly easy to draw them both from

memory. She'd sketched them on the beach, building a sandcastle as they had on that first outing on Kallos. She'd drawn Angelos's face suffused with love, and Sofia's with wonder, both of them working together, drawing pleasure from each other's company. It had felt like a healing, the lancing of a wound, to draw them. Each pencil stroke had been a blessing, and she hoped Angelos would keep the drawing, and see in it the esteem and affection she held for them both.

'So what's wrong with this dress?' she asked Willow, who was moving around her, clucking her tongue.

'Honestly? It looks like a green bin bag,' Willow said frankly, and Talia let out a reluctant laugh. She couldn't help but admire her brother's fiancée's plain speaking. 'Admittedly, a very nice shade of green,' Willow added generously, 'but still.' She shook her head, eyes dancing. 'You have a knockout figure and gorgeous hair, and you don't do much with either.'

'I've never had to,' Talia admitted. Living like a hermit precluded fancy hair, make-up or clothes.

'But today is different, isn't it?' Willow asked. 'It's meant to be special.'

'Yes…'

Willow glanced at the clock on the mantelpiece. 'We have a few hours before the exhibition. Will you let me give you a bit of a makeover? Only if you want to, of course.'

'A makeover?' Talia started to shake her head, inherently resisting the idea, before she paused. Why shouldn't she have a makeover? This was her new start, after all. She wanted to move on. Desperately. 'Sure,' she said, and smiled at Willow. 'Why not?'

He wasn't going to open it. Angelos stared at the plain brown manila envelope postmarked from America and scowled. He didn't want to know what Talia had sent. He didn't care.

It was a lie that was becoming harder and harder to believe, especially considering how much time he'd spent and sleep he'd lost thinking about Talia.

It had been a month since she'd left, an utterly endless thirty days of misery. The new nanny had arrived, and she was just what Angelos had wanted. Once. She was cool and capable and a little bit remote, and while her attention to Sofia was faultless, neither Angelos nor Sofia had been able to warm to her. Her laughter didn't ring through the rooms of the villa; she didn't speak in clumsy, pidgin Greek; she didn't have freckles on her shoulders and sunlight in her hair. She wasn't Talia.

He knew he should forget Talia. She'd lied to him, after all. In the month since she'd left Angelos had vacillated between regret at treating her so harshly and certainty that he'd done the right thing, the only thing. They had no future.

Expelling a low, frustrated breath, Angelos stared at the unopened parcel before him and then, his mouth in a hard line, he slit the envelope.

The paper he drew out was not the letter he'd been expecting. It was a drawing, and when he saw it for what it was his heart clenched hard inside him. He didn't need to see the initials 'TD' in the corner to know it was Talia's work.

Yet what humbled and amazed him was how she'd drawn him. He looked so…loving. Gentle and tender, like the best version of himself, a version he hadn't believed existed before Talia had come into his life. And she'd drawn Sofia with her face alight, her eyes bright with happiness. A slip of paper fell out of the envelope, and frowning, Angelos picked it up. His heart clenched again at the words Talia had written:

*I drew what I saw.*
*This is who you really are.*
—*Talia*

Angelos closed his eyes against the wave of regret that crashed over him. Talia had seen more in him, more hope and love and gentleness, than he'd ever shown her. How was that possible? And what could he do about it now?

He opened his eyes and gazed at the sketch once more, a lump forming in his throat, and then, swallowing it down, he put the drawing back in the envelope and rose from his desk.

'Almost ready.' Willow brushed Talia's face with loose powder before stepping back and examining her handiwork critically, her hands on her hips. 'I think you'll do,' she said with a wink, and Talia lifted one shaky hand to her hair that Willow had subdued into glossy perfection.

'I'm almost afraid to look.'

'And I'm almost insulted by that,' Willow teased. 'Look in the mirror.'

'Okay.' Taking a deep breath, Talia swivelled around in her chair to face the full-length mirror. And gasped in shock. Her usual tangle of golden-brown waves had been pulled into an elegant, smooth chignon. Her figure, usually shrouded by shapeless T-shirts and shorts, was encased in an ice-blue halter-top dress that clung to every slender curve. Matching high-heeled strappy sandals completed the outfit.

'Oh, my goodness,' she whispered. 'I don't think I've ever looked so...'

'Beautiful?' Willow filled in, and Talia let out an uncertain laugh.

'So glamorous. So on display.' She had, she realised,

hidden herself in more ways than one: both on the estate and in shapeless clothes. But she wanted to be different now. She would be different.

She smoothed her hands down the shiny satin of her dress before turning to Willow. 'Thank you. I feel great.'

'And you look great,' Willow said as she kissed her cheek. 'Don't forget it.'

'I won't.'

Most of her family had come for the gallery exhibition, and Talia was both humbled and amazed by their encouragement. She knew how busy everyone was, with her brothers and sisters all involved in some aspect of the Di Sione corporation. She appreciated them taking the time to come and show their support.

She rode to the gallery in her grandfather's limo; Giovanni sat next to her, looking more alert and refreshed than he had in a long time.

'I'm so pleased for you, *cara*,' he said, and patted her knee. Talia smiled back at him.

The gallery was housed in a shingle-roofed cottage by the beach, one wall made entirely of glass overlooking Long Island Sound.

The curator of the exhibit had done a fantastic job hanging her pictures, making the best use of the natural light and airy space. Waiters circulated with trays of canapés and flutes of champagne, and guests, including most of her family, had already arrived.

'Talia!' Her sister Bianca came towards her, arms outstretched.

'Bianca.' Talia hugged her sister; they'd always been close, separated only by a year. 'It's been too long.'

'I know, I know.' Bianca shook her head, blushing, her gaze moving from Talia to a rugged-looking man with sandy hair and ice-grey eyes. 'Liev,' she murmured. 'My fiancé.'

'I can't believe it,' Talia murmured as she hugged her sister again. Bianca let out a shaky laugh and hugged her back. 'I think there's a story behind this,' Talia said, and she laughed again.

'There is. But I'm not going to tell it now.'

'I'll be waiting.' Talia loved seeing her sister looking so happy; joy radiated from her in a way Talia knew she'd felt once, in Angelos's arms. 'I'm so glad you're happy, Bianca,' she said. 'I can tell how much you love him.'

'And he loves me,' Bianca answered. 'Which is amazing in itself—I remember finding a love letter once, between the pages of a book in the library, from someone named Lucia. I don't know who she was, or whom she was writing to, but reading that letter made me wonder what it would feel like to be loved so much. And now I know.'

'Lucia,' Talia repeated in surprise as she thought of the inscription in *Il Libro d'Amore*. 'Do you think…do you think she had something to do with Grandfather?'

'I don't know. He's never told us the real story behind the Lost Mistresses, has he?'

Talia glanced at her grandfather; he was chatting with her brother Matteo, smiling and nodding, and even though he looked better than he had in a long time, he was still tired and frail. 'I hope he tells us sometime,' she said quietly.

Talia continued to circulate among her guests, chatting to her brothers and sisters, enjoying their encouragement and praise. She noticed her half-brother, Nate, standing by a wall, holding a glass of champagne, and she approached him with a hesitant smile.

'Nate, it's been such a long time.'

'It always is,' Nate said with an answering smile and veiled eyes.

'You know you're the only brother I have whose portrait I haven't painted?'

'Half-brother.'

'I don't count by halves.'

His smile deepened and the darkness in his eyes lifted a little. 'I'm glad of that, Talia.'

'Will you sit for me? Please?'

'At the estate?'

'Does that bother you?'

He rubbed his jaw. 'I don't know.'

'Nate…' Talia put a hand on his sleeve. 'You should talk to him,' she said softly, for she'd seen that her brother's gaze had drifted to Giovanni and Matteo talking. 'He doesn't have long, you know. You should reconcile while you can.'

'Maybe,' Nate answered, but he didn't sound convinced.

'He asks after you sometimes,' Talia told him. 'Did you know that?'

Nate's gaze had darkened again and he shook his head. 'No, I didn't.'

'Talk to him,' Talia urged again. She was just turning away to greet another person when she caught a familiar figure in her peripheral vision. Even though she couldn't actually see the person, her body prickled in instinctive awareness and her heart began to beat hard.

Slowly she turned and looked towards the doorway of the gallery, where Angelos stood, his gaze burning into hers.

# CHAPTER SEVENTEEN

'ANGELOS…' HIS NAME slipped from her lips, and she nearly swayed. Angelos strode towards her, the crowds parting before him, and then he was right there in front of her, looking tall and strong and as devastatingly attractive as ever.

'Talia, I'm sorry.'

'No, I'm sorry,' she blurted. 'For not telling you about the book. For leaving the way I did…'

'I let you leave. And I overreacted about the book.' He glanced around the room, every single person's speculative gaze swivelled towards them. 'May we talk in private? For a moment? And then I want to look at all these fabulous portraits, although I think I have the best one by far, back in Kallos.'

'You received the sketch?'

'Yes, and it made me realise how much I'd wilfully threw away. How stupid I was—' He broke off and reached for her hand. 'But let me tell you in private.'

Talia let him lead her outside, down to the beach that wasn't nearly as soft and white as the sand on Kallos, but she didn't care where she was, as long as she was with Angelos.

'Well?' she said, her voice wobbling a bit in trepidation, because even now she wasn't sure what he was going to say. She was afraid to hope, to *believe*… 'Why did you come all the way to New York?'

'To tell you I love you. And I'm sorry for the way I acted over that book.'

'You love me?' An incredulous smile bloomed across her face. 'Really?'

'I think I fell in love with you the first time you stormed into my office and demanded I spend more time with Sofia.'

'You seemed infuriated at the time—'

'I was,' Angelos admitted with a laugh. 'But I admired your strength and courage, and I knew you wanted to do right by my daughter.' He sat down on the sand, tugging her down with him. Talia went, heedless of her satin dress. They sat side by side in the sand, hands linked, savouring being together, before Angelos spoke again. 'I've been afraid, Talia,' he said quietly. 'Afraid of loving someone again, of giving my heart and then getting hurt.' His grip tightened on her fingers. 'I shut Sofia out for that reason, although I convinced myself it was for her benefit. Seeing your sketch of us made me realise how much I've missed, how much I haven't let myself feel. I thought it was because I couldn't, and I told myself I was staying away for Sofia's sake. But the truth is it was for my own. It's easier to build a shell around yourself than let yourself be hurt. I couldn't bear the thought of losing someone again.'

'I know you loved your wife very much, Angelos—'

'I did, but it doesn't mean I can't love again.'

'But when I told you about the book…' Talia swallowed hard. 'I left, at least in part, because I felt like I could never be first in your heart. The way you talked about your wife and the inscription in the book that you shared… I thought there was no way we could have that together.'

'We'll have something different,' Angelos answered, 'and every bit as strong and good. You're different than Xanthe, Talia. You reached me in a way she never did, as much as we loved each other.'

Talia frowned in confusion. 'What do you mean?'

'Xanthe never wanted to hear about my childhood. She wanted to pretend I'd been born a billionaire—I think she was ashamed of my humble roots.'

'But her grandmother was a lady's maid!'

'To a duchess,' Angelos reminded her. 'Everyone has a weakness, and perhaps that was hers. We loved each other, and it was a good marriage, but I am ready to move on. I know I need to, and I want to, with you.' His dark gaze met hers, and Talia ached see the touching uncertainty in his eyes. 'If you'll still have me.'

'Oh, Angelos, of course I will,' she exclaimed, her voice choking. 'I'm the one who should be sorry. I handled the whole thing with the book so wrong. I know I should have told you earlier. You said it's easier to build a shell around your heart—in my case, it was easier simply to run away. You helped me to face my fears but they still defeated me in the last moment. I left because I was hurting and scared, and I couldn't bear being around you while you shut me out. I should have stayed and battled it out.'

'Perhaps we needed some time apart,' Angelos allowed, 'as long as we don't have any more.'

'Never,' Talia agreed, and then to both her relief and joy, he slid his hands to frame her face and kissed her.

The touch of Angelos's lips to her own was a balm to her soul and sent sparks showering through her body. She deepened the kiss, every part of her yearning for him, and Angelos responded in kind. In moments they were both lying on the sand, limbs tangled together as their hands roved and their mouths fused.

Finally Angelos broke apart from her with a shaky laugh. 'I do not want to embarrass myself,' he said, running a hand through his hair as Talia tried to straighten her clothes. 'And I wanted to give you this.' He withdrew a familiar, slim volume from the inside of his jacket and Talia gasped in surprise.

'*Il Libro d'Amore*…but it's so precious to you…'

'And precious to your grandfather, I think, if he wanted it so much.'

'I don't fully understand why,' Talia answered. 'But I think there are many things my grandfather hasn't told me.' She took the book, running her hand along the butter-soft cover. 'But are you sure? I know how much this means to you.'

'You mean more to me, Talia,' Angelos said. 'I want you to give the book to your grandfather. He has only memories left. We have a future, together.'

'Then let's give it to him together,' Talia said, and Angelos smiled ruefully.

'I have not even met him or any of your family yet.'

'I'll introduce you,' she said. 'And then we can give the book to my grandfather. He'll be so pleased, not just to get the book, but to know I am happy with you. He could tell how miserable I was these last few weeks.'

'And so could Sofia with me,' Angelos admitted. 'Maria told me she'd never seen me so grumpy.'

'Now that's saying something,' Talia teased, and with her heart full and singing, she pulled him up from the sand and led him back to the gallery, where the rest of her life waited, ready to unfold.

\* \* \* \* \*

*If you enjoyed this book,
look out for the next instalment of*
THE BILLIONAIRE'S LEGACY:
*A DEAL FOR THE DI SIONE RING*
*by Jennifer Hayward.
Coming next month.*

# MILLS & BOON®

## EXCLUSIVE EXTRACT

Hotel magnate Nate Brunswick's faith in marriage
has been destroyed by his father – but searching
for his beloved grandfather's lost ring leads the
illegitimate Di Sione to an inconvenient engagement!
Mina Mastrantino can only pass the ring on once
she's married. A divorce should be easy…
but their exquisite wedding night gives them
both far more than they planned!

*Read on for a sneak preview of*
A DEAL FOR THE DI SIONE RING
by Jennifer Hayward

"You're an honorable man, Nate Brunswick. *Grazie.*"

"Not so honorable, Mina." A dark glitter entered his
eyes. "You called me improper not so long ago. I can
be that and more. I am a hard, ruthless businessman who
does what it takes to make money. I will turn a hotel
over in the flash of an eye if I don't see the flesh on the
bones I envisioned when I bought it. I will enjoy a
woman one night and send her packing the next when
I get bored of her company. Know what you're getting
into with me if you accept this. You will learn the
dog-eat-dog approach to life, *not* the civilized one."

Why did something that was intended to be a warning
send a curious shudder through her? Mina drew the wrap
closer around her shoulders, her gaze tangling with
Nate's. The glitter in his eyes stoked to a hot, velvet

shimmer as he took a step forward and ran a finger along the line of her jaw. "Rule number one of this new arrangement, should you so choose to accept it, is to not look at me like that, *wife*. If we do this, we keep things strictly business so both of us walk away after the year with exactly what we want."

Her gaze fell away from his, her blood hot and thick in her veins. "You're misinterpreting me."

"No, I'm not." He brought his mouth to her ear, his warm breath caressing her cheek. "I have a hell of a lot more experience than you do, Mina. I can recognize the signs. They were loud and clear in my hotel room that day and they're loud and clear now."

She took a deep, shuddering breath. To protest further would be futile when her skin felt like it was on fire, her knees like jelly. He watched her like a cat played with a mouse, all powerful and utterly sure of himself. "The only thing that would be more of a disaster than this day's already been," he drawled finally, apparently ready to have mercy on her, "would be for us to end up in bed together. So a partnership it is, Mina." He lifted his glass. "What do you say?"

*Don't miss*
**A DEAL FOR THE DI SIONE RING**
by Jennifer Hayward

Available January 2017
www.millsandboon.co.uk